W9-BWV-544

Integrating
Literature, Language and the Arts
Using the Tales of the Brothers Grimm

Written and Illustrated by
Sister Carol Joy Cincerelli, HM

Cover by Sister Carol Joy Cincerelli, HM

Copyright © Good Apple, Inc., 1990

ISBN No. 0-86653-562-4

Printing No. 987654321

Good Apple, Inc.
1204 Buchanan St., Box 299
Carthage, IL 62321-0299

The purchase of this book entitles the buyer to reproduce the student activity pages for classroom use only. Any other use requires the written permission of Good Apple, Inc.

All rights reserved. Printed in the United States of America.

Table of Contents

Introduction iii
Bloom's Taxonomy iv
To the Teacher viii
Jacob and Wilhelm Grimm 1
    Time Line for the Grimm Brothers 4
Folklore 5
Make a Grimm Mobile 6
Germany—East and West 12
    Map of Europe 14
    Map of Germany 15
    Learning More About Germany 16
Wolfgang Amadeus Mozart 17
    Wolfgang Amadeus Mozart's Time Line 19
    The Magic Flute 21
    Some Musical Terms 23
Questions According to Bloom's Taxonomy 24
Introducing the Tales of the Grimm Brothers to Your Students 28
The Frog Prince 31
    The Story and Activities
Rapunzel 37
    The Story and Activities
Ashputtel (Cinderella) 45
    Many Cinderellas 53
    Activities 59
    Spoonerisms 62
    Bibliography of Cinderella Stories 65
    Illustrators of Cinderella 66
Snow White and Rose Red 67
    Activities 77
Hansel and Gretel—Summary 81
    Activities and Puppets 83
Sleeping Beauty—Summary 89
    Activities 91
Little Red Riding Hood—Summary 95
    Activities 96
The Three Spinning Fairies—Summary 103
    Activities 105
The Fisherman and His Wife—Summary 109
    Activities 111
The Golden Goose—Summary 113
    Activities 115
The Elves and the Cobbler—Summary 117
    Activities 118
Task Cards 119
Extending the Lesson 127
The Learning Center 129
Tales from the Brothers Grimm 133
Records of Grimm Tales 134
Award 135
Evaluation 136

CURR
LB
1527
.C86
G75
1990

Copyright © 1990, Good Apple, Inc.

GA1160

Introduction

Children are our hope of the future. The work of education is the well-being of the world's children—to make our existence more meaningful, more productive, more expressive, more caring, more life giving. You, because you are a teacher, are one of the most influential people in the life of each child who passes through your classroom. Striving for educational excellence is a part of your daily objectives—a part of what you wish to accomplish with each child.

Plato noted that the natural laws of governing the structure of the universe—harmony and proportion, balance and rhythm—also govern music, painting, dance; and he urged making these art forms a foundation of the education method.

There was a time when the teaching of children was much easier. Now we are part of a society that is exposed to many interpretations of basic values. We have not taught our children to appreciate and value those wonderfully creative works which speak to our souls. We live in a time when genius is still being expressed in the arts. But emphasis to understanding and appreciating the arts is secondary to the basics instead of a basic. It is the arts that fill us with dreams, hopes and aspirations. The arts are the most natural means by which we express our creativity.

I invite you to use my book, my ideas, my beliefs to assist you in releasing that power to create that lies deep inside each human being.

Sister Carol Joy Cincerelli, HM

"**Since every child is born with the power to create, that power should be released early and developed wisely. It may become the key to joy and wisdom, and possibly to self-realization. Whether or not the child becomes an artist is immaterial.**"

Florence Cane

Copyright © 1990, Good Apple, Inc.

GA1160

Bloom's Taxonomy
Some Thoughts

Dr. Benjamin Bloom's *Levels of Questioning for the Cognitive Domain* is crucial to our understanding of how to formulate higher level thinking skills. Higher level thinking skills are essential to developing an understanding of the arts.

Bloom lists the lowest level of thinking as the one asking for knowledge. "What is the name of the blonde girl in the story of the Three Bears?" is an example. The only answer to that question is "Goldilocks." The question does not challenge, nor does it invite you to think beyond it.

As we move up the Bloom ladder of thinking skills we find questions that ask the child to evaluate. An evaluation question could be, "What do you think the insurance adjuster would say when he came to the home of the three bears to investigate the damage that Goldilocks had done?" Each student could give a different answer and each could be correct. There is no correct answer to the question; rather many answers are possible. There is the potential for greater learning because students would need to listen and evaluate the possibilities.

We must remember whenever factual information is presented to the brain it enters through the left hemisphere. If the information is not used again for the next three days it could be forgotten. The human brain is limited in its capacity to store and recall facts.

When we use right brain activities such as humor, storytelling, art, music, movement and poetry, learning is enhanced and strengthened and passes from the temporary memory of the left brain to the more permanent memory of the right hemisphere. This happens almost automatically when the student is "allowed to use" or is exposed to right brain activities.

Many teachers and school systems do not value these right brain activities and continue to ignore them in order to have more time for factual learning. In reality what they are doing is presenting only half of the educational process, for the process is incomplete and damages a holistic approach to learning and life.

Copyright © 1990, Good Apple, Inc.

GA1160

Stating Behavioral Objectives for Classroom Instruction

Major Categories in the Cognitive Domain of the Taxonomy of Educational Objectives (Bloom, 1956)

Descriptions of the Major Categories in the Cognitive Domain

1. **Knowledge.** Knowledge is defined as the remembering of previously learned material. This may involve the recall of a wide range of material, from specific facts to complete theories, but all that is required is the bringing to mind of the appropriate information. Knowledge represents the lowest level of learning outcomes in the cognitive domain.

2. **Comprehension.** Comprehension is defined as the ability to grasp the meaning of material. This may be shown by translating material from one form to another (words to numbers), by interpreting material (explaining or summarizing), and by estimating future trends (predicting consequences or effects). These learning outcomes go one step beyond the simple remembering of material and represent the lowest level of understanding.

3. **Application.** Application refers to the ability to use learned material in new and concrete situations. This may include the application of such things as rules, methods, concepts, principles, laws, and theories. Learning outcomes in this area require a higher level of understanding than those under comprehension.

4. **Analysis.** Analysis refers to the ability to break down material into its component parts so that its organizational structure may be understood. This may include the identification of the parts, analysis of the relationships between parts, and recognition of the organizational principles involved. Learning outcomes here represent a higher intellectual level than comprehension and application because they require an understanding of both the content and the structural form of the material.

5. **Synthesis.** Synthesis refers to the ability to put parts together to form a new whole. This may involve the production of a unique communication (theme or speech), a plan of operation (research proposal), or set of abstract relations (scheme for classifying information). Learning outcomes in this area stress creative behaviors with major emphasis on the formulation of new patterns or structures.

6. **Evaluation.** Evaluation is concerned with the ability to judge the value of material (statement, novel, poem, research report) for a given purpose. The judgments are to be based on definite criteria. These may be internal (organization) or external criteria (relevant to the purpose), and the student may determine the criteria or be given them. Learning outcomes in this area are highest in the cognitive hierarchy because they contain elements of all of the other categories, plus conscious value judgments based on clearly defined criteria.

Bloom's Taxonomy (Cognitive Domain)

Areas of Taxonomy	Definition	What Teacher Does
1. Knowledge	Recall or recognition of specific information	Directs Tells Shows Examines
2. Comprehension	Understanding of information given	Demonstrates Listens Questions Compares Contrasts Examines
3. Application	Using methods, concepts, principles and theories in new situations	Shows Facilitates Observes Criticizes
4. Analysis	Breaking information down into its constituent elements	Probes Guides Observes Acts as a resource
5. Synthesis	Putting together constituent elements or parts to form a whole requiring original, creative thinking	Reflects Extends Analyzes Evaluates
6. Evaluation	Judging the values of ideas, materials and methods by developing and applying standards and criteria	Clarifies Accepts Harmonizes Guides

Copyright © 1990, Good Apple, Inc.

GA1160

Bloom's Taxonomy (Cognitive Domain)

What Student Does	Process Verbs		Notes
Responds Absorbs Remembers Recognizes	define repeat list name label	memorize record recall relate	
Explains Translates Demonstrates Interprets	restate describe explain identify report tell	discuss recognize express locate relate	

Solves
  problems
Demonstrates
  use of knowledge
Constructs
	translate
	apply
	employ
	use
	practice
	shop
		interpret
		demonstrate
		dramatize
		illustrate
		operate
		schedule	

Discusses Uncovers Lists Dissects	distinguish calculate test criticize debate question	differentiate experiment diagram inspect inventory relate	
Discusses Generalizes Relates Compares Contrasts Abstracts	compose propose formulate assemble construct manage	plan design arrange collect organize prepare	
Judges Disputes Develops criteria	judge evaluate compare score choose estimate predict	appraise rate value select assess measure	

Copyright © 1990, Good Apple, Inc.

GA1160

To the Teacher

This unit of learning has been prepared for your use in an effort to integrate the arts into a more wholistic curriculum that will invite and challenge the child to learn as well as to acquire a growing understanding and appreciation of the arts. This unit incorporates literature, music and the visual arts with basic skills of basic subject areas such as reading, science, math, grammar, social studies and spelling.

The value of the arts to the student can be expressed as the goals or learning outcomes of the lessons and activities in this book. They are

To allow expression
To help strengthen a healthy self-concept
To provide joy in learning
To help build fine and large motor skills
To develop good work habits
To integrate classroom activities

To integrate learning styles into the curriculum
To develop appreciation of self and others
To promote problem-solving skills
To develop decision-making skills
To allow emotions to react
To enhance creative thinking
To develop a sensitivity to beauty

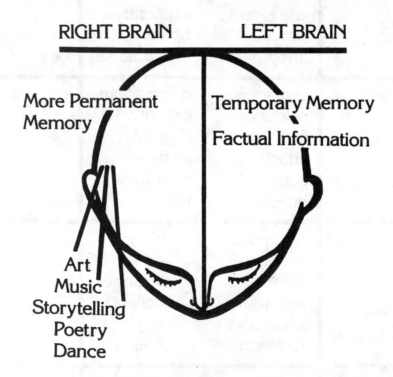

RIGHT BRAIN   LEFT BRAIN

More Permanent Memory

Temporary Memory

Factual Information

Art
Music
Storytelling
Poetry
Dance

"Any educational process that neglects half the brain is half an education at best, at worst, it is the mutilation of human capabilities."

Eliott Eisner

Copyright © 1990, Good Apple, Inc.

GA1160

Jacob and Wilhelm Grimm

The Grimm brothers, Jacob and Wilhelm, were known throughout Germany as language researchers and fairy-tale collectors and have secured an everlasting place in the history of all people.

Jacob Ludwig Grimm was born January 4, 1785, and Wilhelm Karl Grimm February 24, 1786. Together they collected, retold and published the world famous *Grimm's Fairy Tales*. Born in Hanau they spent their school days in Kassel and then went on to the University of Marburg. All their lives they were inseparable.

Together they put down the fundamental principals for German linguistics, began the German encyclopedia and sought out the fairy tales of the German people and recorded them. Today those tales have been translated into many languages and are heard throughout the world.

There were nine children in the Grimm family but only six, Jacob, Wilhelm, Carl, Ferdinand, Ludwig, Emil and Lotte, lived. Their father died before his forty-fifth birthday.

In 1798 the two brothers went to Kassel to stay with an aunt where they attended the Lyceum. They had very little money. The wealthy children treated them with arrogance.

In 1802 and 1803 they began to study law at the University of Marburg. When Jacob was 23, their mother died and he had to provide for the other children with his meager earnings.

After studying at the University of Marburg, Jacob went to Paris and became the librarian of Jerome Bonaparte, King of Westphalia and brother of Napoleon I. In 1829 Jacob became professor of Germanic languages and Wilhelm became the librarian at the University of Gottingen. In 1841 both Jacob and Wilhelm became professors at the University of Berlin.

It is important to remember that the fairy tales Jacob and Wilhelm recorded were not composed by them, as Hans Christian Andersen wrote his own. The Grimm's recorded tales that had been told for hundreds of years and had been passed down by word of mouth.

Copyright © 1990, Good Apple, Inc.

1

GA1160

Except for the year that Jacob worked in Paris, the brothers were never separated. Because they were born only a year apart, they acted very much like twins.

They always loved to hear the German tales. One day they met a friend named Clemens Brentano. This man loved the German past and collected ancient literature. He invited the brothers to write some of their folk songs and published them in his book titled *Wunderhorn.*

Jacob and Wilhelm had their desks side by side so they were together when they worked.

They continued to collect old tales from family and friends and even bartered for tales.

There was an old woman, Marie Muller, who owned a drugstore in Kassel and knew many old stories. Some of her stories were French in origin, but she retold them in German. She gave the brothers many, many stories. Another friend named Achim von Arnim read the tales and encouraged the Grimms to publish them.

The two brothers spent weeks walking about the German countryside in search of the old stories. The Grimm brothers spent most of their time in the old town of Kassel. There they sat in kitchens and gardens and listened to grandmothers tell the stories their grandmothers had told them. They heard such stories as "Hansel and Gretel," "The Goose Girl," "Cinderella" and "Rumpelstiltskin." The Grimm brothers wrote the stories down, and their first collection was published in 1812.

Soon people were bringing them stories and waited for them to publish again.

Only adults read the first book and many found the stories dull. Later, Wilhelm took pains to use the same words the storytelling grandmothers used and made the characters talk in a natural fashion. In this style, the stories became popular with children. The brothers published several volumes of the stories. Today the best of them are usually published in one book and called *Grimm's Fairy Tales.* Jacob Grimm was a language scholar and was interested in the histories of the tales. He saw in them the German survivals of old Greek and Teutonic myths. He showed how the Brynhild of the Teutons had become "Briar Rose" in the modern version, and how "The Poor Man and the Rich Man" was just the old Greek story of Baucis and Philemon.

One day Hans Christian Andersen came to visit them. Wilhelm was not at home and Jacob, who was busy writing, did not recognize him and sent him away. When Wilhelm found out what had happened, he was very embarrassed because Andersen was already a famous writer of fairy tales. But Jacob was working on a German grammar book and did not want to be disturbed.

Copyright © 1990, Good Apple, Inc.

GA1160

When Wilhelm was 39 years old he married Dorothea Wild. They were married on May 15, 1825, and later they had three children: Herman, Rudolf and Auguste. Jacob never married but continued to live with his brother and his family.

They continued to work side by side, take walks together and share brotherly love for the rest of their lives.

They published *German Folk Tales* and many more works. They began work on the first complete dictionary of the German language. This dictionary became the model for dictionaries in many other languages.

When the King of Prussia heard of the dictionary, he invited them to live and work in Berlin and paid for all aid and support as well as a home for the family.

They had become successful and famous. The Grimms have left us many wonderful stories. They may well be the stories that were read to us as we were growing and our imaginations were fresh.

Wilhelm died in 1859 and Jacob died in 1863. They are remembered with love throughout the world.

Copyright © 1990, Good Apple, Inc.

GA1160

Time Line for the Grimm Brothers

A time line is a sequential listing of important events in a person's life. This time line begins on the day that a person is born and ends with his death. The important events in order of when they happen are points on that time line.

The time line for Jacob Grimm begins in 1785 and for Wilhelm in 1786.

1785—Jacob Grimm born in Hanau, Germany

1786—Wilhelm Grimm born in Hanau, Germany

1796—Jacob and Wilhelm's father dies of pneumonia at age 44

1798—The brothers move to Kassel

1802-3—They begin to study law at the University of Marburg

1806—Napoleon's army conquers Germany

1808—Jacob becomes librarian to Jerome Bonaparte, King of Westphalia

1812—First volume of *Grimm's Fairy Tales* published

1812—Napoleon's army is defeated in Russia

1814—Wilhelm joins Jacob as librarian

1816—First two volumes of German legends published

1825—Wilhelm marries Dorothea Wild

1828—Jacob publishes *Study of Old Teuton Laws*

1829—Jacob becomes professor of Germanic language

1830-37—Both are professors at Kassel

1841—Both brothers become professors at University of Berlin

1859—Wilhelm's death

1863—Jacob's death

Have your students research what historical events took place during the lifetime of the Grimm brothers. Each event discovered could be printed on an index card and pinned to a clothesline hung in the classroom.

Folklore

The folklore of a nation is really the traditions and customs of its people. Because for hundreds of years there was no way of printing the written word and because few people could read or write, these customs and traditions were handed down from generation to generation by mouth and performance.

In many countries it was the duty of the parents and grandparents to inform the children of the family's, community and nation's past. Stories, dances, art, music, games, costumes and religion are all a part of a people's folklore.

There are several kinds of folklore—these include:

1. Myths
2. Fables
3. Legends
4. Fairy Tales

Myths are closely related to religion and they are stories that explain life and death and the great forces of nature. Every group of people had these stories to explain things, like the stars or moon, that they did not understand.

Fables are stories that teach people how they should live. Most fables are about animals and have a moral at the end of each story. The fables we know best today are those collected by a Greek slave named Aesop. They are called *Aesop's Fables.*

Legends are stories that teach and may be partly true. Most tell about people who really lived. The famous stories of King Arthur and the Knights of the Round Table are legends.

Fairy Tales are stories handed down or written today that entertain us and take place in a make-believe place. Many times supernatural characters appear such as fairies or a godmother who has magical powers.

In the United States we have *Indian Folklore* told by many tribes of Indians early in our country's history.

Copyright © 1990, Good Apple, Inc.

GA1160

Make a Grimm Mobile

There are twelve pieces to the Grimm mobile. The first is the name plate which is the profile of the Grimm brothers.

From that drawing all the story circles will hang.

1. Paint or color each of the pieces.

2. Cut them out.

3. Glue each to a piece of tagboard to give it support.

4. When gluing the story circles, you may want to put one on one side of the tagboard circle and one on the other.

5. If you have access to a laminator, laminate the pieces.

6. Attach the pieces together with heavy-duty thread or invisible fish line which can be purchased at a variety store.

7. Hang the mobile from a light fixture or some prominent spot in the classroom.

You may choose to make the Grimm brothers mobile the focal point of a learning center you create in the corner of your classroom. Many of the ideas in this book are ready to use in a learning center. Later in the book you will find work sheets, task cards as well as suggestions for an easy-to-create learning center.

Copyright © 1990, Good Apple, Inc.

6

GA1160

Jacob and Wilhelm

GRIMM

On the back side of this mobile piece you may wish to print the birth and death dates of the Grimm brothers. You may choose to print any other significant information. Since the mobile could possibly be seen from both sides, you may choose to glue two of this piece back to back or on each side of a piece of tagboard. This can be done for all of the mobile pieces.

Copyright © 1990, Good Apple, Inc.

GA1160

Jacob and Wilhelm Grimm

Jacob   Wilhelm

Copyright © 1990, Good Apple, Inc.

8

GA1160

The Frog Prince

Rapunzel

Cinderella

Snow White & Rose Red

Copyright © 1990, Good Apple, Inc.

9

Copyright © 1990, Good Apple, Inc.

10

GA1160

The Fisherman and His Wife

The Golden Goose

The Elves and The Cobbler

Copyright © 1990, Good Apple, Inc.

11

Germany

In order to better understand the lives of Jacob and Wilhelm Grimm, we should look at the country from which they came.

During the time that the brothers were alive, Germany was not a divided country as it is today. During the 1500's it was the center of the Reformation, and some of the world's finest philosophers, musicians, authors and scientists hailed from this great country.

Early accounts tell us that the ancient Germans were tall and fair. They were country people who raised animals and lived in tribes. In fact, their history was not recorded for years because they wandered through the forests of northern Europe. As Germany progressed, education became of prime importance to the people as it is today. Due to this fact many German people have been recognized for their great contributions to the world especially in the arts and sciences.

In both World War I and World War II, Germany was accused of starting the war, and other countries united together to defeat them. Since World War II Germany has been divided into two countries: West and East Germany. These countries are very different even though the people themselves share so much in common.

West Germany is the larger of the two having the city of Bonn as its capital. It is a democratic republic and has three times the number of people as East Germany. It has many natural resources and is mostly industrial.

West Germany

Copyright © 1990, Good Apple, Inc.

GA1160

Children there are tested for their special academic gifts or talents and in the fifth grade are sent on to schools that specialize in their areas. If the tests show that the child has no special ability, he remains in the elementary program and later attends a vocational school.

The Communist party controls East Germany. The capital city is East Berlin and it is mostly an agricultural country. The Communists have strict legislation over the schools in order to ensure that the Communist principles are taught.

It appears that there will be great changes taking place in the two Germany's because of political decisions made in late 1989. The Communist leaders of East Germany have, at least for a while, lessened their control over the people. East Germans are now free to leave East Germany. Many are. This is creating many problems for both East Germany and West Germany. But it appears that after forty-five years the two Germany's have the opportunity to be more like one country.

Germany has many famous universities that are hundreds of years old.

German people are known for being exact and thorough in their work. They take great pride in what they do.

They are a Teutonic people which means their language includes German, English, Dutch, Flemish and the Scandinavian languages. Those people in northern Germany are generally fair with light eyes while those in the south are darker and rounder.

Knowing these facts about German people helps us to understand how hard working and intense the Grimm brothers were in all their writings.

East Germany

Copyright © 1990, Good Apple, Inc.

GA1160

Europe

Use a red marker or crayon and outline all of Germany both East and West.

Color East Germany yellow and West Germany green.

Color democratic nations of Europe orange and Communist nations of Europe blue.

Locate the cities of Berlin and Bonn.

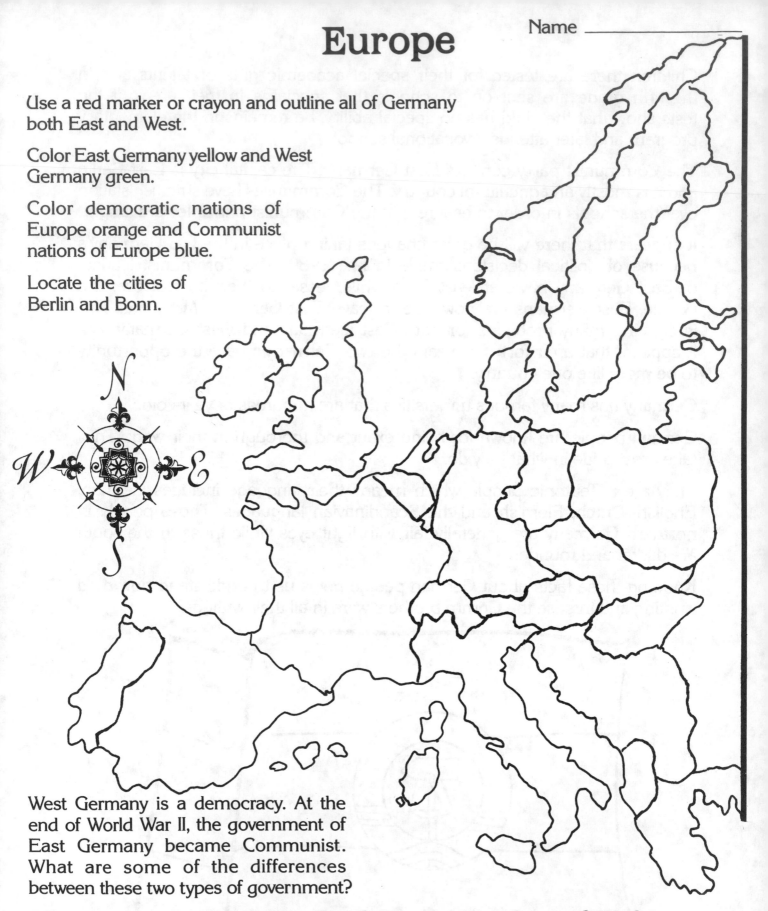

West Germany is a democracy. At the end of World War II, the government of East Germany became Communist. What are some of the differences between these two types of government?

Where do you think life is better—East Germany or West Germany? Why? In what ways do you think life is better?

Do you think the Grimm brothers could have lived and written their fairy tales if Germany had been communistic when they lived?

Copyright © 1990, Good Apple, Inc. 14 GA1160

Use this map for activities on the following page.

Name _____

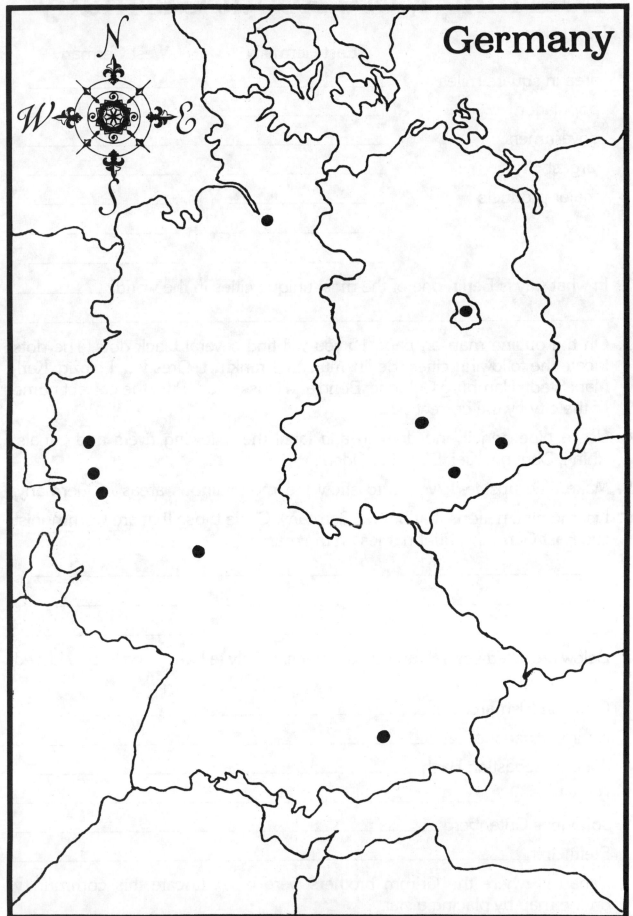

Germany

Copyright © 1990, Good Apple, Inc.

GA1160

Learning More About Germany

1. East versus West

	East Germany	West Germany
area in square miles	_____	_____
population	_____	_____
government	_____	_____
largest city	_____	_____
major products	_____	_____
	_____	_____
	_____	_____

2. In what way is Berlin one of the most unique cities in the world?_____
_____

3. On the outline map on page 15 you will find several black dots. The dots locate the following cities: Berlin, Munich, Frankfurt, Dresden, Leipzig, Karl-Marx-Stadt, Hamburg Cologne, Bonn and Dusseldorf. Print the correct name of the city by the correct dot.

4. Use a blue pencil and draw in and label the following rivers and canals: Rhine, Danube, Kiel, Elbe and Oder.

5. Make little upside-down *v's* to show the mountainous areas of Germany.

6. List the nine nations that border Germany. Circle those that are Communist like East Germany. Print names on the map.

_____   _____   _____

_____   _____   _____

_____   _____   _____

7. Below are listed several famous Germans. Briefly tell why each is considered to be famous.

Otto von Bismarck _____

Konrad Adenauer _____

Johann Sebastian Bach _____

Boris Becker _____

Johannes Gutenberg _____

Steffi Graf_____

8. Hanau is where the Grimm brothers were born. Locate this community on the map by placing a star.

Copyright © 1990, Good Apple, Inc.

GA1160

Wolfgang Amadeus Mozart

(1756-1791)

Throughout its history Germany has been the home of many talented people. Even though Wolfgang Amadeus Mozart was born in Salzburg, Austria, his family had its roots in Germany. Mozart was living at the time the brothers Grimm were born.

Born on January 27, 1756, Wolfgang was the second child of Leopold Mozart who was a violinist in the band of the archbishop of Salzburg. His mother's name was Anna Marie Pertl Mozart and his older sister's name was Marianne. Marianne began taking harpsichord lessons when Wolfgang was three and he could play the same pieces that she was learning. Because of these musical abilities, he was known as the "wonder child" when he was still quite young.

At the age of 4 Wolfgang's father began giving him music lessons and he began composing music. He was soon recognized as a genius. His father took him on tour and he performed perfectly. Everyone was amazed that a child so young could know so much. Everywhere people bestowed presents on him.

Even as a young child he had a beautiful face and clear blue eyes. He was not a spoiled child and was ready to laugh and have fun.

Before he was ten he visited Munich and Vienna where he played the clavier, violin and organ for the royal court. Sometimes he even did this with his eyes closed. He toured Europe and in London played for the king and queen of England. While in London he took singing lessons and began composing symphonies.

At the age of 10 he returned to Salzburg. Four years later his father took him to Italy. While there he heard the Pope's choir and memorized the music of the Miserere. He was deeply moved by the religious music he heard. In Italy he was commissioned to write an opera.

At the age of 21 Wolfgang and his mother went to Paris. His father had to stay in Salzburg and work. On the way to Paris he gave many concerts. While in Paris his mother became ill and died and he had to return to Salzburg. There he continued to write music.

In 1782 he married a young woman named Constanze Weber (1763-1842). They lived in Vienna. It was during these years that Mozart wrote the operas *The Marriage of Figaro* and *Don Giovanni*. They were both successful but earned him little money. To help a friend, Wolfgang began writing his last opera *The Magic Flute*. It was at this time at this early age that Mozart began feeling ill. He was also almost broke.

He began work on a *Requiem* (Mass for the Dead) and became almost obsessed with it. Early in the morning of December 5, 1791, he died. He was only thirty-five years old. Because he and his wife had no money for burial, his body was put in a large grave for the poor. At that time several poor people were laid to rest in the same grave. That is why we do not know where he is buried.

Constanze was left with two young sons to raise. Mozart left his young family with little, but he left the world for generations to come so much wonderful music. In his short thirty-five years of life, he composed over 600 works including operas, operettas, cantatas, church music, 39 litanies, 48 symphonies, 33 serenades, 29 orchestral sets and 41 collections of dances.

We must be grateful that Wolfgang Amadeus Mozart shared his gift with the world. It does not seem fair that his life ended so soon or that he was poor. Many times people who are considered to be a genius suffer a great deal.

Wolfgang's son Karl Thomas (1784-1858) was a gifted pianist. His second son, Franz Xaver Wolfgang (1791-1844), was a composer, pianist and music conductor.

Copyright © 1990, Good Apple, Inc.

GA1160

Wolfgang Amadeus Mozart's Time Line

1756—Born on January 27 at Salzburg, son of Leopold Mozart, court musician, and Anna Marie Pertl Mozart.

1760—Begins lessons on clavier with his father.

1761—Composes his first pieces: Minuet and Trio in G Major, Andante for Piano

1762—On tour with his father and sister Nannerl to Munich and Vienna.

1763—Begins study of the violin with his father. Goes on concert tour of German cities, Brussels, and Paris.

1764—Makes concert appearances in Paris. Visits London where he plays before George III. Composes symphonies and sonatas.

1765—Travels from London to Holland, back to Paris and then to Switzerland, Munich and finally home to Salzburg.

1767—Embarks on second visit to Vienna.

1768—In Vienna, Emperor Joseph II commissions opera *Lafinta semplice*. First opera, *Bastien and Bastienne*, is composed and performed.

1770—Has a triumphal tour of Italy. His first of three.

1773—Returns from Italy to Salzburg. Goes to Vienna in search of a court appointment. Returns to Salzburg and produces string quintet.

1774—Composes bassoon concerto. Leaves for Munich in December.

1775—Opera *Lafinta giardiniera* is produced in Munich. Composes five violin concertos, among them the No. 4 in D Major.

1776—Returns to Salzburg where there is growing friction with his employer, the archbishop.

Copyright © 1990, Good Apple, Inc.

GA1160

1778—Has an emotional entanglement with Aloysia Weber. Finally departs for Paris, where his mother becomes ill and dies.

1779—Back in Salzburg, he accepts a position from the archbishop.

1780—Opera *Ideomeneo* is commissioned and finally finished.

1781—*Ideomeneo* is produced in Munich. Mozart goes to Vienna; leaves the archbishop's service. Resides with the Weber family.

1782—Marries Constanze Weber in Vienna.

1783—Visits Salzburg with Constanze. Composes string quartet No. 15 in D Minor.

1784—A son, Karl Thomas, is born.

1785—Begins work on *The Marriage of Figaro*.

1786—*The Marriage of Figaro* is produced in Vienna and in Prague, where it is a huge success.

1787—Visits Prague, where his symphony No. 38 in D Major is performed. *Don Giovanni* is commissioned. Mozart meets Beethoven. *Don Giovanni* is produced. Mozart is appointed to compose for the Viennese court by Joseph II.

1788—Composes three of his greatest symphonies

1789—Goes on tour to Leipzig, Berlin, Dresden and Prague.

1790—Joseph II dies. His successor, Leopold, fails to appoint Mozart to this court.

1791—Despite ill health, he is obsessed with composing: string quintets in D Major and E Flat Major, piano concerto in B Flat, clarinet concerto in A Major. The *Requiem* is commissioned by Count Franz von Walsegg. *The Magic Flute* is produced. Mozart works feverishly, but his condition deteriorates. With the *Requiem* unfinished, he dies.

Copyright © 1990, Good Apple, Inc.

GA1160

The Magic Flute

An Opera in Two Acts
by Wolfgang Amadeus Mozart

The opera of *The Magic Flute* was one of Mozart's last works. Many consider it a great miracle. Mozart was tired, poor and depressed in the last year of his life. He was not sure writing this opera was a good idea, but he needed the money and wanted to write again for the German people. The original work is written in German.

Act I

Prince Tamino is hunting and is found by a huge snake. He is so terrified he falls unconscious and is saved by three Ladies of the Queen of the Night. They kill the snake and inform the queen of the Prince's presence. He awakens and finds Papageno, a birdcatcher, who captures birds for the queen. The Prince thinks Papageno has killed the snake. When the birdcatcher doesn't deny it, he is punished.

The three Ladies return and present the Prince with a small portrait of the queen's daughter Pamina, who has been taken away by the evil Sarastro.

The queen sees that the Prince is taken with the daughter's beauty and promises her to him when she is free. The ladies give the Prince a magic flute to protect him from danger. The birdcatcher goes with the Prince to free the queen's daughter. The three Ladies give him a magic chime of silver bells.

Papageno reaches Sarastro's palace and the birdcatcher frees the princess and tells her of Prince Tamino's love for her. She goes to look for the Prince.

As the Prince approaches the Temple of Wisdom he learns that Sarastro is not wicked as the queen has said. He is confused as he leaves the temple. The birdcatcher and princess enter, just missing him. They are pursued by Monostatos and his slaves. They are saved when the birdcatcher rings his magic chime of bells.

Just then Sarastro finds them and says, although he cannot set the princess free yet, salvation lies in escape from her mother.

The Prince is brought in and he and Pamina embrace. Next the Prince and birdcatcher must go through trials of purification to reach his goal.

Act II

The priests assemble near the temple and Sarastro says the gods have destined the Prince and Pamina as husband and wife. She must be protected by Prince Tamino from her evil mother.

Copyright © 1990, Good Apple, Inc.

GA1160

Sarastro hears of the plan. The princess begs pity for her mother and Sarastro assures her that vengeance is not in his heart.

Tamino and Papageno are sworn to silence when Pamina finds them and realizes the prince will not speak to her, she thinks he doesn't love her anymore and she wants to die.

She takes her mother's dagger and is about to kill herself when she is stopped by the three Genii and is told that the prince does love her.

Tamino must go through more tests, and he and Pamina greet each other as two lovers. Together, with the help of the magic flute, the two survive the ordeal of passing through caverns of fire and water.

The lonely Papageno wants someone to love him. He sets his magic chimes pealing and soon the pretty Papageno joins him.

At that point, the Queen of the Night and her three ladies come for revenge. A terrible storm comes up and swallows them up in the earth.

A brilliant light illuminates the scene and Sarastro is surrounded in all his glory by Pamina, Tamino and the priests.

He hails the victory of the powers of light over the forces of darkness. There is great rejoicing.

Copyright © 1990, Good Apple, Inc.

GA1160

Some Musical Terms

THE OPERA

The opera is a dramatic story told in song with orchestral accompaniment. It began in the sixteenth century in Italy, was developed largely in Italy and France and emerged in its present form with the "dialogue" between songs delivered in a chanting style known as recitative. A familiar part of any opera is the aria where the characters express their moods and feelings. Some of the most colorful singing is known as coloratura where the soloist sings long passages on a single syllable with soaring trills.

THE SYMPHONY

In the history of music, the symphony has become the most important form of all. In early days the name was applied to many different styles of composition, but the generally accepted form now is a work of four movements.

A typical symphony starts with an allegro—a movement in quick tempo. This is followed by a slow movement. Next comes a minuet, and the final movement is another allegro.

THE COMPOSER

The person who has written the music for the opera or symphony as Mozart did is called the composer.

THE ORATORIO

Oratorio is an Italian word meaning "chapel" or "house of prayer." In Rome in the sixteenth century, scenes from the Scriptures were enacted in chapels. Music was a part of this, so the term began to be applied to the music itself. Later, in history the oratorio was performed on a concert platform without acting and scenery. That is why most oratorios have a religious theme. George Frideric Handel is recognized as being the greatest composer of this style of music.

THE CONDUCTOR

In former times it was always necessary for someone to "give the time" to a group of players because written music was not then divided into bars. In more modern times the conductor began to do far more than beat time. He was responsible for the way in which an orchestra interpreted the music and the prominence to be given to one group of instrumentalists at any part of the work.

With various positions of his baton, the conductor can indicate the exact tempo and volume he wants from an orchestra. The left hand is also used to give directions to the players.

Copyright © 1990, Good Apple, Inc.

GA1160

Questions According to Bloom's Taxonomy

Knowledge

Name the country that the Grimm brothers and Mozart were from.

Why are Jacob and Wilhelm Grimm famous?

Why is Mozart famous?

In what year was each of these three men born?

Comprehension

What was exceptional in the life of the Grimms?

Why was Mozart exceptional?

Who had an easier life, the Grimms or Mozart?

Why was their work important?

Application

Dramatize Mozart conducting *The Magic Flute.*

If Mozart was such a genius and everyone loved his music, why did he die so poor?

Demonstrate the Grimms interviewing the peasants and recording their stories. Illustrate that scene.

Use the outline map of Europe found on page 14 and the time line of Mozart's life found on pages 19-20 and locate on the map the places where Mozart lived or performed.

Copyright © 1990, Good Apple, Inc.

GA1160

Questions According to Bloom's Taxonomy

Analysis

Make a list of all the musical instruments you would need to form your own orchestra.

Compare the fairy tales collected by the Grimms to those written by Hans Christian Andersen. Which do you prefer and why?

Listen to several selections of Mozart's music. How does the music make you feel? Can you imagine him writing this music?

How do you feel about such a famous man being buried in a grave for the poor?

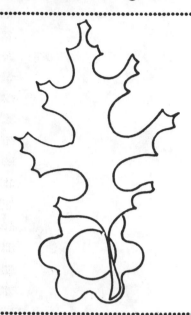

Synthesis

Collect and record personal stories told by your family members. Write them down as part of your family history.

Find out what kind of music each member of your family likes best and why. Would it have been easier or more difficult for Mozart to become famous if he had not become so well known as a child?

Why do most stories set obstacles to be overcome in the way of happiness? What is a hero? Who is the hero in *The Magic Flute*?

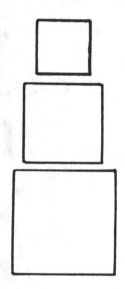

Evaluation

If you had been Mozart's older sister, would you be happy that he was so talented and people everywhere praised him, or would you feel resentful because you could play well too and did not receive the same acclaim?

How is the symbol of light conquering darkness like good conquering evil in fairy tales?

If you had been Jacob and Wilhelm Grimm, how would you help people understand the importance of the work you were doing in collecting fairy tales?

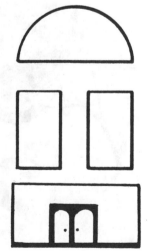

Copyright © 1990, Good Apple, Inc.

GA1160

From Jacob and Wilhelm

THE FROG-PRINCE

TO YOU

Copyright © 1990, Good Apple, Inc.

The following stories by the Grimm brothers have been selected for inclusion in this book. You will find either the story told or a summary. There are many others and a little research will enable you to expand on those presented.

The Three Spinning Fairies
Snow White and Rose Red
The Elves and the Cobbler
Fisherman and His Wife
Little Red Riding Hood
Hansel and Gretel
The Golden Goose
Sleeping Beauty
The Frog Prince
Ashputtel
Rapunzel

Copyright © 1990, Good Apple, Inc.

GA1160

Introducing the Tales of the Grimm Brothers to Your Students

In this book you will find much information. There is background information about the Grimm brothers, Wolfgang Amadeus Mozart and his work. You will also find many work sheets, task cards, ideas for a learning center and an abundance of illustrations and patterns. There are time lines, questions for discussion, questions and activities based on Benjamin Bloom's thinking skills. But the important question now is how to start. Only you know what will work best with your students, and you know that one group of learners must be dealt with differently than another. However, here are some suggestions.

Possibility #1

Choose your favorite tale by the Grimm brothers and read it to your students. Share the illustrations in the book you choose with your students.

When finished, ask the students if that is how they remember the story. What was different? What was new? What was learned?

Possibility #2

Ask your students if they remember the story of "Hansel and Gretel." You could use any of the more familiar stories. Have the students tell the class what is remembered. Put the basic story together piece by piece. One student's thought will awaken another's memory. When all information seems to be present, read a version of the story to your students.

Discuss what details were forgotten. Discuss how these details add images to the story.

Have a student begin telling the story once again. After a few lines, allow another student to continue telling the story. Proceed until the story is completed.

Possibility #3

Tell, don't read, your favorite story by the Grimm brothers to your students. Actually select a lesser known story. When you are finished, hand out a list of other stories by the brothers. Ask each student to choose one. Allow the students a day or two to refresh their memories of their stories to find versions in the library.

Group students according to the story selected. If ten select the same story, divide this group into two groups. Let the groups work and compare versions found.

Each group will in the end tell the rest of the class the story they have chosen. Each child will tell a part.

Copyright © 1990, Good Apple, Inc.

GA1160

Possibility #4

Relate to your students some information about the Grimm brothers, their lives and their times. Present the mobile pieces that relate to them. Ask students to recall any of their stories. As they do, add the mobile circle pertaining to that story.

Then present any remaining mobile pieces and give a one or two-sentence summary of that story. With the motivational mobile hanging in place, you are now ready to begin your study of the fairy tales by the Grimm brothers.

A Final Thought

Several stories and a vast amount of accompanying material is presented in this book. It is there for you to use and omit. In no way is there any intention for you to use all the material presented. Choose what is appropriate for the age of your students. Adapt any other ideas. Eliminate that which is not appropriate.

Best wishes and have fun.

Copyright © 1990, Good Apple, Inc.

GA1160

Basic Concepts

Stories	Themes
The Frog Prince	Be careful what you promise. A promise must be kept.
Rapunzel	You cannot imprison something just for yourself. A little knowledge is a dangerous thing.
Cinderella	Hard work develops character. Search for what you love.
Snow White and Rose Red	Kindness is rewarded. It is better to love than to fear.
Hansel and Gretel	It is better to solve a problem together rather than alone. Sorrow will be replaced with joy.
Sleeping Beauty	Perseverance wins the crown. Time cannot dim true love.
Little Red Riding Hood	Be truthful and do not deceive. Be kind to your elders.
The Three Spinning Fairies	A talent should be used. The truth is better than a lie.
The Fisherman and His Wife	Simplicity in living is best. Greed is never satisfied.
The Golden Goose	Looks may be deceiving. Laughter is a gift.
The Elves and the Cobbler	Labor is love in action. One good turn deserves another.

Copyright © 1990, Good Apple, Inc.

30

GA1160

The Frog Prince

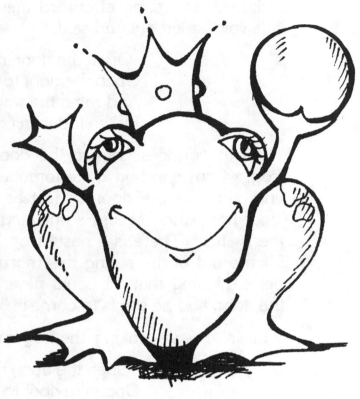

One fine evening a young princess put on her bonnet and clogs and went out to take a walk by herself in a wood; and when she came to a cool spring of water that rose in the midst of the woods, she sat herself down to rest a while. Now she had a golden ball in her hand, which was her favorite plaything, and she was always tossing it up into the air and catching it again as it fell. After a time she threw it up so high that she missed catching it as it fell, and the ball bounded away and rolled along upon the ground till at last it fell down into the spring. The princess looked into the spring after her ball, but it was very deep, so deep that she could not see the bottom of it. Then she began to bewail her loss, and said, "Alas! if I could only get my ball again I would give all my fine clothes and jewels, and everything that I have in the world."

Whilst she was speaking, a frog put its head out of the water and said, "Princess, why do you weep so bitterly?" "Alas!" said she, "what can you do for me, you nasty frog? My golden ball has fallen into the spring." The frog said, "I want not your pearls and jewels and fine clothes; but if you will love me, and let me live with you and eat from off your golden plate, and sleep upon your bed, I will bring you your ball again." "What nonsense," thought the princess, "this silly frog is talking! He can never even get out of the spring to visit me, though he may be able to get my ball for me, and therefore I will tell him he shall have what he asks." So she said to the frog, "Well, if you will bring me my ball, I will do all you ask." Then the frog put his head down, and dived deep under the water; and after a little while he came up again with the ball in his mouth and threw it on the edge of the spring. As soon as the young princess saw her ball, she ran to pick it up; and she was so overjoyed to have it in her hand again that she never thought of the frog but ran home with it as fast as she could. The frog called after her, "Stay, Princess, and take me with you as you said." But she did not stop to hear a word.

Copyright © 1990, Good Apple, Inc.

GA1160

The next day, just as the princess had sat down to dinner, she heard a strange noise—tap, tap-plash, plash—as if something was coming up the marble staircase, and soon afterward there was a gentle knock at the door and a little voice cried out and said:

> "Open the door, my princess, dear,
> Open the door to thy true love here!
> And mind the words that thou and I said
> By the fountain cool, in the greenwood shade."

Then the princess ran to the door and opened it, and there she saw the frog, whom she had quite forgotten. At this sight she was sadly frightened, and, shutting the door as fast as she could, came back to her seat. The king, her father, seeing something had frightened her, asked her what was the matter. "There is a nasty frog," said she, "at the door that lifted my ball for me out of the spring this morning. I told him that he could live with me here, thinking that he could never get out of the spring; but there he is at the door, and he wants to come in."

While she was speaking, the frog knocked again at the door, and said:

> "Open the door, my princess, dear,
> Open the door to thy true love here!
> And mind the words that thou and I said
> By the fountain cool, in the greenwood shade."

Then the king said to the young princess, "As you have given your word you must keep it; so go and let him in." She did so, and the frog hopped into the room, and then straight on—tap, tap-plash, plash—from the bottom of the room to the top, till he came up close to the table where the princess sat. "Pray lift me upon a chair," said he to the princess, "and let me sit next to you." As soon as she had done this, the frog said, "Put your plate nearer to me that I may eat out of it." This she did, and when he had eaten as much as he could, he said, "Now I am tired; carry me upstairs, and put me into your bed." And the princess, though very unwilling, took him up in her hand and put him upon the pillow of her own bed, where he slept all night long. As soon as it was light he jumped up, hopped downstairs, and went out of the house. "Now, then," thought the princess, "at last he is gone, and I shall be troubled with him no more."

But she was mistaken for when night came again she heard the same tapping at the door, and frog came once more and said:

> "Open the door, my princess, dear,
> Open the door to thy true love here!
> And mind the words that thou and I said
> By the fountain cool, in the greenwood shade."

Copyright © 1990, Good Apple, Inc.

GA1160

And when the princess opened the door, the frog came in and slept upon her pillow as before, till the morning broke. And the third night he did the same. But when the princess awoke on the following morning she was astonished to see, instead of the frog, a handsome prince, gazing on her with the most beautiful eyes she had ever seen, and standing at the head of her bed.

He told her that he had been enchanted by a spiteful fairy, who had changed him into a frog, and that he had been fated so to abide till some princess should take him out of the spring and let him eat from her plate and sleep upon her bed for three nights. "You," said the prince, "have broken this cruel charm, and now I have nothing to wish for but that you should go with me into my father's kindgom, where I will marry you and love you as long as you live."

The young princess, you may be sure, was not long in saying "yes" to all this; and as they spoke a gray coach drove up, with eight beautiful horses decked with plumes of feathers and golden harness; and behind the coach rode the prince's servant, faithful Heinrich, who had bewailed the misfortunes of his master until his heart had well-nigh burst.

They then took leave of the king, and got into the coach with eight horses, and all set out, full of joy and merriment, for the prince's kindgom which they reached safely; and there they lived happily a great many years.

Copyright © 1990, Good Apple, Inc.

GA1160

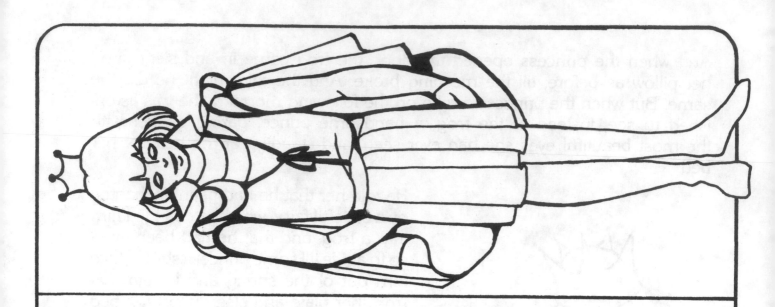

This first picture shows the frog.

The third picture shows the prince.

In the middle space, draw the frog changing into the prince.

Remember to show parts of the frog as well as parts of the prince.

Copyright © 1990, Good Apple, Inc.

34

GA1160

What's in a Promise?

What is a promise?

What promise did the princess make to the frog?

Is it important to keep promises?

How is the Bill of Rights a promise?

Is it ever okay to break a promise? When?

Copyright © 1990, Good Apple, Inc.

35

GA1160

Make a Quilt of the Frog Prince

Materials Needed:

    25-10" fabric squares (smooth cotton with a little polyester)
    fabric for backing
    soft polyester batting for between the squares and backing
    acrylic paints
    brushes
    thin point permanent black markers
    water cups

1. Each child receives a 10" square of fabric and sketches a part of the story of the Frog Prince in pencil.

2. The child outlines the drawing in permanent black marker.

3. With newspaper underneath the fabric, the child then paints the drawing (paint may be thinned with water but not too thin or it will bleed on the fabric).

4. After the paint has dried, outline again with permanent marker.

5. When all squares are finished, teacher or students arrange the pieces in an appealing design of pictures and either hand sew or sew together on a sewing machine.

When the squares are all together, sew front (the squares) to the back fabric making sure the right side is facing in so it can be turned right side out when it is finished. Sew only three of the sides. Turn right side out and fill with batting.

After filling, sew up the fourth side.

The quilt may be used as a wall hanging to remind the children of the Frog Prince.

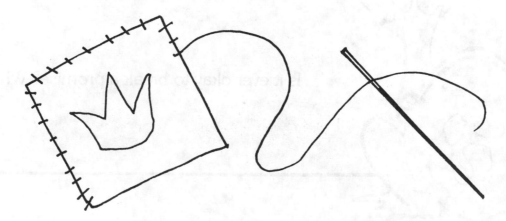

Copyright © 1990, Good Apple, Inc.

GA1160

Rapunzel

There once lived a man and his wife who long wished for a child, but in vain. Now there was at the back of their house a little window which overlooked a beautiful garden full of the finest vegetables and flowers; but there was a high wall all around it, and no one ventured into it, for it belonged to a witch of great might, and of whom all the world was afraid. One day as the wife was standing at the window and looking into the garden, she saw a bed filled with the finest rampion, and it looked so fresh and green that she began to wish for some, and at length she longed for it greatly. This went on for days, and, as she knew she could not get the rampion, she pined away, and grew pale and miserable. Then the man was uneasy, and asked: "What is the matter, dear wife?" "Oh," answered she, "I shall die unless I can have some of that rampion that grows in the garden at the back of our house to eat." The man, who loved her very much, thought to himself: "Rather than lose my wife, I will get some rampion, cost what it will."

So in the twilight he climbed over the wall into the witch's garden, plucked hastily a handful of rampion, and brought it to his wife. She made a salad at once, and ate of it to her heart's content. But she liked it so much, it tasted so good, that the next day she longed for it thrice as much as she had done before. If she was to have any rest, the man must climb over the wall once more. So he went in the twilight again; and as he was climbing back he saw, all at once, the witch standing before him, and was terribly frightened as she cried with angry eyes: "How dare you climb over into my garden like a thief and steal my rampion? It shall be the worse for you!"

Copyright © 1990, Good Apple, Inc.

37

GA1160

"Oh," answered he, "be merciful rather than just. I have only done it through necessity, for my wife saw your rampion out of the window and became possessed with so great a longing that she would have died if she could not have had some to eat."

The witch said, "If it is all as you say, you may have as much rampion as you like, on one condition. The child that will come into the world must be given to me. It shall go well with the child, and I will care for it like a mother."

In his distress of mind, the man promised everything; and when the time came when the child was born, the witch appeared, and, giving the child the name Rapunzel (which is the same as rampion), she took it away with her.

Rapunzel was the most beautiful child in the world. When she was twelve years old, the witch shut her up in a tower in the midst of a wood, and it had neither steps nor door, only a small window above. When the witch wished to be let in, she would stand below and would cry:

"Oh, Rapunzel, Rapunzel! Let down your hair!"

Rapunzel had beautiful long hair that shone like gold. When she heard the voice of the witch, she would undo the fastening of the upper window, unbind the plaits of her hair, and let it down twenty ells below, and the witch would climb up by it.

After they had lived thus a few years, it happened that as the King's son was riding through the wood, he came to the tower; and as he drew near he heard a voice singing so sweetly that he stood still and listened. It was Rapunzel in her loneliness trying to pass away the time with sweet songs. The King's son wished to go in to her, and sought to find a door in the tower, but there was none. So he rode home, but the song had entered into his heart, and every day he went into the wood and listened to it. One day, as he was standing there under a tree, he saw the witch come up, and listened while she called out:

"Oh, Rapunzel, Rapunzel! Let down your hair."

Then he saw how Rapunzel let down her long tresses, and how the witch climbed up by it and went in to her, and he said to himself, "Since that is the ladder, I will climb it and seek my fortune." And the next day, as soon as it began to grow dusk, he went to the tower and cried:

"Oh, Rapunzel, Rapunzel! Let down your hair."

And she let down her hair, and the King's son climbed up by it. Rapunzel was greatly terrified when she saw that a man had come in to her, for she

Copyright © 1990, Good Apple, Inc.

38

GA1160

had never seen one before; but the King's son began speaking so kindly to her and told how her singing had entered into his heart, so that he could have no peace until he had seen her himself. Then Rapunzel forgot her terror, and when he asked her to take him for her husband, she saw that he was young and beautiful. She thought to herself, "I certainly like him much better than old Mother Gothel," and she put her hands into his hands, saying, "I would willingly go with thee, but I do not know how I shall get out. When thou comest, bring each time a silken rope, and I will make a ladder, and when it is quite ready I will get down by it out of the tower, and thou shalt take me away on thy horse." They agreed that he should come to her every evening, as the old woman came in the daytime. So the witch knew nothing of all this until once Rapunzel said to her unwittingly. "Mother Gothel, how is it that you climb up here so slowly, and the King's son is with me in a moment?"

"Oh, wicked child!" cried the witch. "What is this I hear? I thought I had hidden thee from all the world, and thou hast betrayed me!"

In her anger she seized Rapunzel by her beautiful hair, struck her several times with her left hand, and then grasping a pair of shears in her right—snip, snip—the beautiful locks lay on the ground. And she was so hard-hearted that she took Rapunzel and put her in a waste and desert place, where she lived in great woe and misery.

The same day on which she took Rapunzel away, she went back to the tower in the evening and made fast the severed locks of hair to the window-hasp, and the King's son came and cried:

"Rapunzel, Rapunzel! Let down your hair."

Copyright © 1990, Good Apple, Inc.

GA1160

Then she let the hair down, and the King's son climbed up, but instead of his dearest Rapunzel he found the witch looking at him with wicked, glittering eyes.

"Aha!" cried she, mocking him, "you came for your darling, but the sweet bird sits no longer in the nest and sings no more; the cat has got her, and will scratch out your eyes as well! Rapunzel is lost to you, and you will see her no more."

The King's son was beside himself with grief, and in his agony he sprang from the tower; he escaped with life, but the thorns on which he fell put out his eyes. Then he wandered blind through the wood, eating nothing but roots and berries, and doing nothing but lament and weep for the loss of his dearest wife.

So he wandered several years in misery until at last he came to the desert place where Rapunzel lived with her twin children that she had borne, a boy and a girl. At first he heard a voice that he thought he knew, and when he reached the place from which it seemed to come, Rapunzel knew him, and fell on his neck and wept. And when her tears touched his eyes they became clear again, and he could see with them as well as ever.

Then he took her to his kingdom, where he was received with great joy, and there they lived long and happily.

Copyright © 1990, Good Apple, Inc.

40

GA1160

Questions on the Story of Rapunzel

KNOWLEDGE

1. Make a list of things Rapunzel could do in the tower.
2. What words rhyme with *hair, prince, gold, tower, witch*?
3. How many names can you think of that end in *el*?

COMPREHENSION

1. What are the things that come between the cottage kitchen and the rampion patch?
2. Without the use of a ladder, what are the possible ways you can think of to release Rapunzel?

APPLICATION

1. Make a rampion salad. What would you put in it?
2. You are on a committee to determine ways of getting the baby Rapunzel away from the witch and back to her parents. How many ways can you think of to do this?

ANALYSIS

1. How many ways can you think of to measure the height of the tower?
2. In what ways can you say that the witch was poor?
3. Suppose you are living during the years Rapunzel was in the tower and someone told you about her. What kind of article would you publish in the newspaper about the situation?

SYNTHESIS

1. How is the tower like an egg?
2. Looking from the tower window, how would Rapunzel describe what the world looked like? Draw a picture of what Rapunzel sees.

EVALUATION

1. How is Rapunzel's hair like a loom?
2. How would you feel if you were the tower Rapunzel was locked in? How would you feel if you were the witch, the prince, Rapunzel?
3. Suppose you could have anything you wanted without having to pay for it. What five things would you want?
4. You can have great beauty if you swallow a tiny capsule. What would you do? And why?

Copyright © 1990, Good Apple, Inc.

GA1160

A Rapunzel Puppet

1. Paint or color her with pencils, crayons or markers and glue her to a piece of stiffer paper.
2. Tape a tongue depressor or thin dowel rod to the back of the puppet face.
3. Add golden yarn to cover her hair. This you can make very long.
4. Pretend you are Rapunzel talking to one of the following: your mother, your father, the witch, the King's son, Barbara Walters. Write what you would say. Holding your hand puppet, talk to a classmate pretending to be the person you chose.

Copyright © 1990, Good Apple, Inc.

42

GA1160

Help the Prince find Rapunzel.

Copyright © 1990, Good Apple, Inc.

GA1160

Twins

Below are outlines of Rapunzel's twins. One twin is a boy, the other a girl. Name each child. Draw the faces. Add detail to the clothing and color. Cut out. Be sure to complete the back side. All completed children will be used as part of a classroom display.

Copyright © 1990, Good Apple, Inc.

44

GA1160

Ashputtel (Cinderella)

The wife of a rich man fell sick; and when she felt that her end drew nigh, she called her only daughter to her bedside, and said, "Always be a good girl, and I will look down from heaven and watch over you." Soon afterward she shut her eyes and died, and was buried in the garden; and the little girl went every day to her grave and wept, and she was always good and kind to all about her. And the snow fell and spread a beautiful white covering over the grave; but by the time the spring came and the sun had melted it away again, her father had married another wife. This new wife had two daughters of her own that she brought home with her; they were fair in face but foul at heart, and it was a sorry time for the poor little girl. They took away her fine clothes and gave her an old gray frock and laughed at her.

She was banished to the kitchen. There she was forced to do hard work: to rise early before daylight, to bring the water, to make the fire, to cook, and to wash. In the evening when she was tired, she had no bed to lie down on, but was made to lie by the hearth among the ashes; and as this, of course, made her dusty and dirty, they called her Ashputtel.

It happened once that her father was going to the fair and asked his wife's daughters what he should bring them. "Fine clothes," said the first. "Pearls and diamonds," cried the second. "Now, child," said he to his daughter, "what will you have?" "The first twig, dear father, that brushes against your hat when you turn your face to come homeward," said she. Then he bought for the first two the fine clothes and pearls and diamonds they had asked for; and on his way home, as he rode through a green copse, a hazel twig brushed against him and almost pushed off his hat; so he broke it off and brought it away; and when he got home he gave it to his daughter. Then she took it and went to her mother's grave and planted it there and cried so much that it was watered with her tears, and there it grew and became a fine tree. Three times every day she went to it and cried, and soon a little bird came and built its nest upon the tree and talked with her and watched over her and brought her whatever she wished for.

Copyright © 1990, Good Apple, Inc.

45

GA1160

maiden ran out at the back door into the garden, and cried out:

"Hither, hither, through the sky,
Turtledoves and linnets, fly!
Blackbird, thrush and chaffinch gay,
Hither, hither, haste away!
One and all come help me quick!
Haste ye, haste ye—pick, pick, pick!"

Then first came two white doves, flying in at the kitchen window; next came two turtledoves; and after them came all the little birds under heaven,

Now it happened that the king of that land held a feast, which was to last three days; and out of those who came to it his son was to choose a bride for himself. Ashputtel's two sisters were asked to come; so they called her up and said, "Now comb our hair, brush our shoes, and tie our sashes for us, for we are going to dance at the king's feast." Then she did as she was told, but when all was done she could not help crying, for she thought to herself she should so have liked to have gone with them to the ball; and at last she begged her mother very hard to let her go. "You, Ashputtel," she said, "you who have nothing to wear, no clothes at all, and who cannot even dance—you want to go to the ball?" And when she kept on begging, she said at last, to get rid of her, "I will throw this dishful of peas into the ash-heap, and if in two hours' time you have picked them all out, you shall go to the feast, too."

Then she threw the peas down among the ashes, but the little

chirping and fluttering in; and they flew down into the ashes; and the little doves stooped their heads down and set to work, pick, pick, pick; and then the others began to pick, pick, pick; and among them all they soon picked out all the good grain and put it into a dish, but left the ashes. Long before the end of the hour, the work was quite done, and all flew out again at the windows.

Copyright © 1990, Good Apple, Inc.

46

GA1160

Then Ashputtel brought the dish to her mother, overjoyed at the thought that now she should go to the ball. But the mother said, "No, no! You have no clothes and cannot dance; you shall not go." And when Asputtel begged very hard to go, she said, "If you can in one hour's time pick two of these dishes of peas out of the ashes you shall go, too." So she shook two dishes of peas into the ashes.

But the little maiden went out into the garden at the back of the house, and cried out as before:

"Hither, hither, through the sky,
Turtledoves and linnets, fly!
Blackbird, thrush and chaffinch gay,
Hither, hither, haste away!
One and all come help me quick!
Haste ye, haste ye—pick, pick, pick!"

Then first came two white doves in at the kitchen window; next came two turtledoves; and after them came all the little birds under heaven, chirping and hopping about. And they flew down into the ashes; and the little doves put their heads down and set to work, pick, pick, pick; and then the others began, pick, pick, pick; and they put all the good grain into the dishes, and left all the ashes. And then Ashputtel took the dishes to her mother, rejoicing to think that she should now go to the ball. But her mother said, "It is all of no use; you cannot go; you have no clothes and cannot dance, and you would only put us to shame," and off she went with her two daughters to the ball.

Now when all were gone, and nobody left at home, Ashputtel went sorrowfully and sat down under the hazel tree, and cried out,

"Shake, shake, hazel tree,
Gold and silver over me!"

Copyright © 1990, Good Apple, Inc.

GA1160

Then her friend the bird flew out of the tree, and brought a gold and silver dress for her, and slippers of spangled silk; and she put them on and followed her sisters to the feast. But they did not know her and thought it must be some strange princess, she looked so fine and beautiful in her rich clothes; and they never once thought of Ashputtel, taking it for granted that she was safe in the dirt.

The king's son soon came up to her, and took her by the hand and danced with her and no one else, and he never left her hand; but when anyone else came to ask her to dance, he said, "This lady is dancing with me."

Thus they danced till a late hour of the night; and then she wanted to go home; and the king's son said, "I shall go and take care of you to your home," for he wanted to see where the beautiful maiden lived. But she slipped away from him, unawares, and ran off toward home; and as the prince followed her she jumped up into the pigeon-house and shut the door. Then he waited till her father came home, and told him that the unknown maiden who had been at the feast had hid herself in the pigeon-house. But when they had broken open the door they found no one within; and as they came back into the house, Ashputtel was lying, as she always did, in her dirty frock by the ashes, and her dim little lamp was burning in the chimney. For she had run as quickly as she could through the pigeon-house and on to the hazel tree, and had there taken

Copyright © 1990, Good Apple, Inc.

48

GA1160

off her beautiful clothes and put them beneath the tree, that the bird might carry them away, and had lain down again amid the ashes in her little gray frock.

The next day when the feast was again held, and her father, mother, and sisters were gone, Ashputtel went to the hazel tree and said,

"Shake, shake, hazel tree,
Gold and silver over me!"

And the bird came and brought a still finer dress than the one she had worn the day before. And when she came in it to the ball, everyone wondered at her beauty; but the king's son, who was waiting for her, took her by the hand and danced with her; and when anyone asked her to dance, he said as before, "This lady is dancing with me."

When night came she wanted to go home; and the king's son followed her as before, that he might see into what house she went; but she sprang away from him all at once into the garden behind her father's house. In this garden stood a fine large pear tree full of ripe fruit; and Ashputtel, not knowing where to hide herself, jumped up into it without being seen. Then the king's son lost sight of her and could not find out where she was gone, but waited till her father came home, and said to him, "The unknown lady who danced with me has slipped away, and I think she must have sprung into the pear tree." The father thought to himself, "Can it be Ashputtel?" So he had an ax

Copyright © 1990, Good Apple, Inc.

49

GA1160

brought; and they cut down the tree, but found no one upon it. And when they came back into the kitchen, there lay Ashputtel among the ashes; for she had slipped down on the other side of the tree and carried her beautiful clothes back to the bird at the hazel tree, and then put on her little gray frock.

The third day, when her father and mother and sisters were gone, she went again into the garden, and said,

"Shake, shake, hazel tree,
Gold and silver over me!"

Then her kind friend the bird brought a dress still finer than the former one, and slippers which were all of gold, so that when she came to the feast no one knew what to say, for the wonder at her beauty; and the king's son danced with nobody but her; and when anyone else asked her to dance, he said, "This lady is my partner, sir."

When night came she wanted to go home; and the king's son went with her, and said to himself, "I will not lose her this time," but, however, she again slipped away from him, though in such a hurry that she dropped her left gold slipper upon the stairs.

The prince took the shoe and went the next day to the king, his father, and said, "I will take for my wife the lady that this gold slipper fits." Then both the sisters were overjoyed to hear it; for they had beautiful feet, and had no doubt that they could wear the golden slipper. The eldest went first into the room where the slipper was and wanted to try it on, and the mother stood by. But her great toe could not go into it, and the shoe was altogether much too small for her. Then the mother gave her a knife, and said: "Never mind, cut it off; when you are queen you will not care about toes; you will not want to walk." So the silly girl cut off her great toe, and thus squeezed on the shoe, and went to the king's son. Then he took her for his bride, and set her beside him on his horse, and rode away with her homeward.

But on their way home they had to pass by the hazel tree that Ashputtel had planted; and on the branch sat a little dove singing:

"Back again! Back again! Look to the shoe!
The shoe is too small and not made for you!
Prince! Prince! Look again for thy bride,
For she's not the true one that sits by thy side."

Then the prince got down and looked at her foot; and he saw by the blood that streamed from it, what a trick she had played him. So he turned his horse round and brought the false bride back to her home, and said; "This is not the right bride; let the other sister try and put on the slipper." Then she went into the room and got her foot into the shoe, all but the heel, which was too large. But her mother squeezed it in till the blood came, and took her to the king's son; and he set her as his bride by his side on his horse and rode

Copyright © 1990, Good Apple, Inc.

GA1160

Copyright © 1990, Good Apple, Inc.

51

GA1160

away with her.

But when they came to the hazel tree the little dove sat there still, and sang:

"Back again! Back again! Look to the shoe!
The shoe is too small and not made for you!
Prince! Prince! Look again for thy bride,
For she's not the true one that sits by thy side."

Then he looked down and saw that the blood streamed so much from the shoe that her white stockings were quiet red. So he turned his horse and brought her back again. "This is not the true bride," said he to the father. "Have you no other daughters?" "No," said he. "There is only a little dirty Ashputtel here, the child of my first wife; I am sure she cannot be the bride." The prince told him to send her. But the mother said, "No, no she is much too dirty; she will not dare show herself." However, the prince would have her come; and she first washed her face and hands, and then went in and curtsied to him, and he reached her the golden slipper. Then she took her clumsy shoe off her left foot, and put on the golden slipper; and it fitted her as if it had been made for her. And when he drew near and looked at her face he knew her, and said, "This is the right bride." But the mother and both the sisters were frightened and turned pale with anger as he took Ashputtel on his horse and rode away with her. And when they came to the hazel tree,

the white dove sang:

"Home! Home! Look at the shoe!
Princess, the shoe was made for you!
Prince! Prince! Take home thy bride,
For she is the true one that sits by thy side!"

And when the dove had done its song, it came flying and perched upon her right shoulder, and so went home with her.

Copyright © 1990, Good Apple, Inc.

GA1160

Many Cinderellas

Fairy tales are traditional tales that have been handed down from generation to generation by word of mouth. These tales go back into the mists of time, through centuries that we can only sum up with the term *oral tradition.* Whenever fairy tales are told, some part of the story usually changes. These changes produce many variants which are very interesting and educational.

Although most fairy and folk tales were handed down to us by the telling of the stories, they were one of the first kinds of stories to be put into print.

In France, Charles Perrault recorded eight fairy tales for adults; "Puss in Boots," and "Cinderella" were included. Folklorists analyze folk tales according to motifs or patterns. Scholars have found versions of "Cinderella" in ancient Egypt, in China in the ninth century, and in Iceland in the tenth century. Still today we find "Cinderella" being told and retold, some versions more appealing than others.

According to the research of Kris Gehrs there is universal sympathy for the girl who loses her mother and acquires an evil stepmother. Cinderella is good; the stepmother is bad, and in the end, the girl is rewarded for her goodness. It is said that there are over nine hundred versions of the Cinderella tale throughout the world. We can examine six versions: German, French, Italian, Jewish, Vietnamese and Icelandic. The characters, settings, plot and types of enchantment differ; however the underlying themes are the same.

No one can say for sure where the oral tale of "Cinderella" began. It first surfaced in literary form in ninth century China. Then in 1697 the story was included in Charles Perrault's collection of folk tales called *Tales of Mother Goose* or *Contes de Ma Mere Loye* and also in his collection entitled *Histories ou Contes du temps passé* as "Cendrillon." Prior to this, however, the Italian Straparola had a similar story. In any event, whenever the tale is told, the teller brings to the tale something of his or her culture.

Out of France came the version of Cinderella that is most enchanting, as was France during the Romantic movement. Marcia Brown's interpretation of Charles Perrault's "Cinderella" differs from other tales in that Cinderella has a fairy godmother who grants

Copyright © 1990, Good Apple, Inc.

53

her wishes. Her godmother, with her magical wand, transforms a pumpkin into a carriage, six mice into horses, a rat into a coachman and six lizards become footmen. Cinderella's rags change into a beautiful gown. Her identity is revealed by the glass slipper. She forgives her sisters who come to live with her and end up marrying two lords of the court.

The Grimm brothers' tale "Ashputtel" was recorded in Germany from the time 1785-1863. The Grimms' tale of "Cinderella" differs from Perrault's version in both plot and mood. When Cinderella's mother dies, she tells Cinderella to be "devout and good. God will always help you and I will look down upon you from heaven, and watch over you." The tale is filled with religious symbolism and beliefs characteristic of the strength of Christianity of Germans during this time in history.

Much discussion could generate from this version; however the question of whether or not this version is too violent for children has been raised. The stepsisters cut off their toes and heels in an effort to fit their feet into the golden shoe. Additionally, doves peck out the stepsisters' eyes as punishment for their wickedness leaving them blind. Despite this fact, Nonny Hogrogian illustrates and retells the Grimms' version in a lovely picture book that is non-threatening for children.

One version of "Cinderella" from Italy has authentic Italian flavor. Cenerentola meets her prince at a feast where they serve pasta, pastry, macaroni and sweetmeat. This Cinderella's father marries a governess who has six daughters. Cenerentola's wishes are granted from the Dove of the Fairies in the Island of Sardinia and from a date tree.

A Jewish version of "Cinderella" entitled "The Exiled Princess" has a few unexpected twists to the plot. The princess has no name in the story. She becomes a servant to a rabbi, his wife and son. The princess marries the son, whom she meets at a Jewish wedding. The king later regrets having expelled the princess and is reunited with her at the circumcision of the grandson. All go with the king back to the palace to live, including the rabbi and his wife. The king reigns in the palace, the princess is able to give to the poor, and the rabbi and his son spend the rest of their lives studying the Torah.

Tam is also mistreated in Vietnam by a cruel stepmother and discovered by a prince (thanks to a slipper) in "The Brocaded Slipper." The reader learns many things regarding Vietnamese tradition. For example, the crow, or phoenix, which steals Tam's slipper and drops it at the prince's feet is one of four mythical creatures. It is the symbol of happiness and good fortune. Next, the prince discovers Tam after asking an old woman the question of who prepared the betel that they chewed. Betel chewing is still seen as a custom

Copyright © 1990, Good Apple, Inc.

55

GA1160

in Vietnam mostly among the older generation. It is a social custom and in olden times it was a perfect way to get acquainted especially with someone of the opposite sex. Furthermore, it is noteworthy to know when reading this tale that instead of commemorating birthdays, the Vietnamese celebrate death days of their relatives, especially parents and grandparents. Beyond that, the Vietnamese belief in afterlife should be researched in conjunction with reading this tale. Tam is repeatedly destroyed by her stepmother and stepsister. First her spirit flies off in the form of an oriole; then the bones grow into two peach trees and finally become a persimmon which falls into a basket, thus saving her and enabling her to return to human form.

The natural background of "The Golden Shoe" is truly Icelandic. It is one of the few tales that has come out of Iceland that is suitable for children. The stark realities of the island of ice and fire are generally not gentle or whimiscal. In "The Golden Shoe" we meet Kari whose father sails to Greenland. Kari spends time watching the Northern Lights. It is against her religion to eat horse meat. When Kari and her horse run away, they cross fields of polar bears, yokuls (ice mountains) and geysers. The twist to this plot is that although a chieftain falls in love with Kari, Kari says she will never love him because as a maid he scorned her but as a princess he admired her. The spell of her faithful friend, Sleipner her horse, is broken because of Kari's trust. He becomes Norwood, a handsome young man of fine stature. The two marry and live happily on a farm working, playing and loving.

Consequently, through these and other folk tales of "Cinderella," children can broaden their understanding of the world. Children are able to see that human needs, problems and feelings are universal. Equally important, children develop an appreciation for the culture of different countries. Some tales provide children with factual information such

Copyright © 1990, Good Apple, Inc.

GA1160

as food, government, family patterns and celebrations. Likewise, children become familiar with different languages, vocabulary words and dialects of the world. And finally, children realize that all people have inherent qualities of goodness, mercy, courage and industry. The tales of "Cinderella" are no exception. Cruelty, fantasy, love, forgiveness, punishment, beauty, slavery and belonging feel the same in all parts of the world by all people. Regardless of a child's roots, it is not hard to relate to Cinderella.

The names of Cinderella in tales varies just as the story itself varies.

Cendrillon	France
Ashputtel (The Grimm Brothers)	Germany
Tattercoats	England
Tam	Vietnam
Shih Chieh	China
Turkey Girl	Zuni Indian
Rhodopis	Egypt
Pepelnica	Croatian
Vasilisa	Russia
Cenerentola	Italy

In "Cinderella" by the Grimm brothers, Cinderella wishes to go to the ball; however her wicked stepmother tells her, "I have emptied a dish of lentils into the ashes for you. If you can pick them out within two hours, you shall be able to go to the ball with us." By this statement it is clear to the reader that the stepmother is not very nice, but rather mean and wicked. The stepsisters are just as mean as the mother. They boss Cinderella to comb their hair, brush their shoes, fasten their buckles, and then turn around and laugh at her. Although the stepmother and stepsisters are not physically described, the reader is able to see their true character through their sayings and actions.

In the version we are most familiar with, Cinderella is asked to wait on her stepmother and stepsisters. But in other cultures she is asked to do such menial tasks as plant rice plants, pick peas out of the ashes, obtain a light from a witch, herd turkeys, wash and scrub the hearth and weave linen.

As children, we remember her fairy godmother coming to rescue her, but in other countries it is not her fairy godmother but a magical pipe, a glowing skull, an enchanted bird, a magical fish, an angel from heaven, a hazel tree or a gooseherd who help Cinderella.

It is exciting to compare all the Cinderellas.

Copyright © 1990, Good Apple, Inc.

GA1160

Copyright © 1990, Good Apple, Inc.

58

GA1160

Design a beautiful coach for Cinderella.

When you have finished, choose Tam from Vietnam, Shih Chieh from China, Turkey Girl (Zuni Indian), Rhodopis from Egypt, Vasilisa from Russia or Cenerentola from Italy. Show through an illustration how this Cinderella might have arrived at the ball. What would pull her coach? Would her coach be a rickshaw, camel caravan, gondola? You decide.

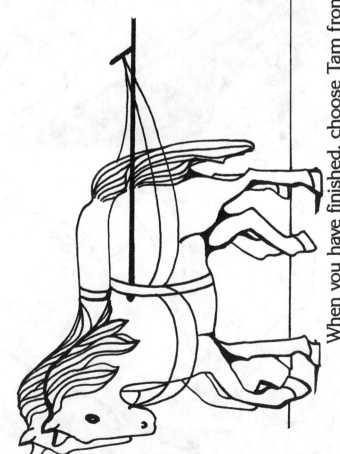

Copyright © 1990, Good Apple, Inc.

GA1160

Who's Shoe?

On the reverse side of this sheet, describe the person who would wear each of the shoes pictured below. What do they do while wearing the shoe? Where do they live? Would they be at the ball? If so, what would they be doing?

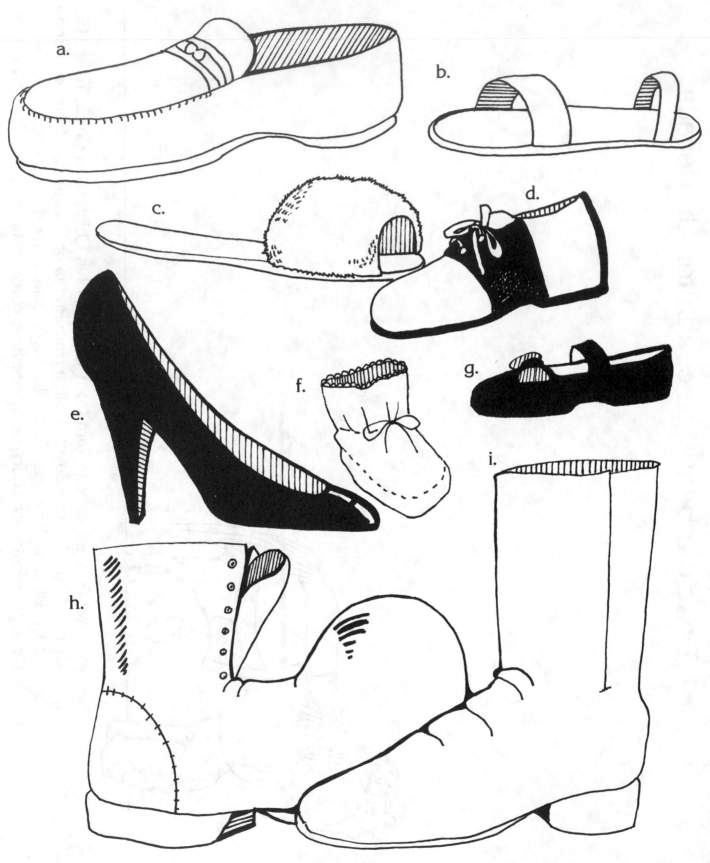

a.

b.

c.

d.

e.

f.

g.

h.

i.

Copyright © 1990, Good Apple, Inc.

60

GA1160

The Castle Grounds

Pretend you are a bird flying above the castle and grounds. Draw the castle and surrounding area as it would appear.

Copyright © 1990, Good Apple, Inc.

61

GA1160

Spoonerisms

The Reverend William Archibald Spooner (1844-1930) was at one time Warden of New College, Oxford. He is known for mixing up the letters in a group of words and consequently mispronouncing them. Some of his mistakes are very entertaining.

Once, when officiating at the wedding of a young couple, he thought he was helping the groom by telling him, "Son, it is customary to cuss the bride." Here are a few more examples. See if you can understand what Dr. Spooner was trying to say:

"I like to ride on a well-boiled icicle."
"The man delivered a blushing crow."
"Young man, you hissed my mystery lecture."
"Mardon me, Padame, this is occupied. May I sew you to another sheet?"

The following are Spoonerisms of the titles of familiar fairy tales. Can you determine the correct titles?

The Loose That Gaid the Olden Geggs _____

_____

The Tare and the Hortise _____

_____

Back and the Stean Jalk _____

_____

Wink Van Ripple _____

_____

Little Ride Hooding Red _____

_____

Loldygocks and the Bee Threars _____

_____

The Ellmaker and the Shooves _____

_____

Ali Theeve and the Forty Babas _____

_____

The Shoolf in Cleep's Woathing _____

_____

Copyright © 1990, Good Apple, Inc.

GA1160

Spoonerism: Prinderella and the Cince

Twonce upon a wime, there was a gritty little pirl named Prinderella who lived with her two sugly isters and her sticked weptmother, who made her pine the shots and shans and do all the other wirty dirk around the house.

One day the ping issued a kroclamation saying that all geligible irls were invited to the palace for a drancy fess ball. The two sugly isters and the sticked weptmother were going, but Prinderella couldn't go because she didn't have a drancy fess. But along came Prinderella's gairy fodmother and changed a cumpkin into a poach and hice into morses, and changed Prinderella's rirty dags into a drancy fess. She sent Prinderella off to the palace saying, "Don't forget to come home at the moke of stridnight."

So Prinderella went to the ball and pranced all night with the cince. At the moke of stridnight, she ran down the stalace peps and on the bottom pep she slopped her dripper! Wasn't that a shirty dame? Well, the next day the ping issued another kroclamation saying that all geligible irls were to sly on the tripper. The two sugly isters and the sticked weptmother slied on the tripper but it fidn't dit. Prinderella slied on the tripper and it fid dit. So, Prinderella and the cince mot garried and hived lappily ever after.

An adaptation of "Prinderella and the Cince" taken from the book *My Tale is Twisted* by Taylor, 1946, no longer in print.

Copyright © 1990, Good Apple, Inc.

63

GA1160

Translating English into English

The wonderful story of Cinderella has been rewritten in spooneristic language. Below you will find some phrases from the spooneristic version.

First, practice reading each phrase as it is written.
Second, translate and write each phrase in English.

1. A gritty little pirl named Prinderella

   _____

2. Her two sugly isters and her sticked weptmother

   _____

3. Changed Prinderella's rirty dags into a drancy fess

   _____

4. Don't forget to come home at the moke of stridnight.

   _____

5. She pranced all night with the cince.

   _____

6. She ran down the stalace peps and on the bottom pep she slopped her dripper.

   _____

   _____

7. They mot garried and hived lappily ever after.

   _____

8. A drancy fess ball

   _____

9. Prinderella's gairy fodmother

   _____

10. It fidn't dit.

    _____

Pick up a copy of the spooneristic version of Cinderella and enjoy reading. Choose any other fairy tale by the brothers Grimm and try writing it in spoonerisms.

Copyright © 1990, Good Apple, Inc.

GA1160

Bibliography of Cinderella Stories

Bierhorst, John *The Glass Slipper: Charles Perrault's Tales of Times Past*. Translated by Charles Perrault. Illustrated by Mitchell Miller. New York: Four Winds Press, 1981.

Brown, Marcia. *Cinderella*, Translated and illustrated by Brown, New York: Charles Scribner and Sons, 1954.

Disney, Walt. *Cinderella*. New York: Random House, 1974.

Dundes, Alan, ed. *Cinderella, a Casebook*. New York: Garland, 1983.

Ehrlich, Amy. *Cinderella*. Translated by Charles Perrault. Illustrated by Susan Jeffers. New York: Dial, 1985.

Evans, C.S. *Cinderella*. Translated by Charles Perrault. Illustrated by Arthur Rackman. New York: Viking Press, 1972.

Galdone, Paul. *Cinderella*. Translated by Charles Perrault. New York: McGraw-Hill, 1978.

Goode, Diane. *Cinderella*. Translated by Charles Perrault. New York: Alfred A. Knopf, 1988.

Haviland, Virginia. *Favorite Fairy Tales Told Around the World*. Translated. Illustrated by S.D. Schindler. Boston: Little, Brown & Co., 1985.

Hogrogian, Nonny. *Cinderella*. Translated by the Brothers Grimm. New York: Greenwillow Books, 1981.

Jeffers, Susan. *Cinderella*, retold by Amy Ehrlich, New York: Dial Books for Young Readers, 1985.

Lucas, Mrs. Edgar. *Sixty Fairy Tales of the Brothers Grimm*. Translated by the Brothers Grimm. Illustrated by Arthur Rackman. New York: Crown, 1979.

Norton, Donna E. *Through the Eyes of a Child*. Second Edition. Columbus: Merrill, 1987.

Perrault, Charles. *Cinderella*. Illustrated by Errol LeCain. New York: Bradbury Press, 1972.

Schwartz, Howard. *Elijah's Violin & Other Jewish Fairy Tales*. Translated. Illustrated by Lindal Heller. New York: Harper & Row, 1983.

Sperry, Margaret. *Scandinavian Stories*. Illustrated by Jenny Williams. New York: Franklin Watts, Inc., 1971.

Tatar, Maria. *The Hard Facts of the Grimm's Fairy Tales*. New Jersey: Princeton University Press, 1987.

Vuong, Lynette Dyer. *The Brocaded Slipper and Other Vietnamese Tales*. Illustrated by Vo-Dinh Mai. Massachusetts: Addison-Wesley, 1982.

Illustrators of Cinderella

The following is a partial list of illustrators of the folk tale "Cinderella." Some of your students will enjoy examining, comparing and contrasting the illustrations of several artists.

Illustrator	Book Title	Version	Copyright	Comments
Brown, Marcia	*Cinderella*	Perrault	1954	Delicate line and color suggesting magical setting
Jeffers, Susan	*Cinderella*	Perrault	1985	Brilliant paintings; fine line pen with ink and dyes
Galdone, Paul	*Cinderella*	Perrault	1987	Large picture book
Goode, Diane	*Cinderella*	Perrault	1988	Beautiful illustrations in vibrant colors
Hogrogian, Nonny	*Cinderella*	Grimm brothers	1981	Lovely illustrated version. Borders, shading, soft colors. Picture book.
LeCain, Errol	*Cinderella*	Perrault	1972	Black and white, and color. Borders, shapes, reflection. Magical transformation depicted.
Rackman, Arthur	*Cinderella*	C.S. Evans (first published in 1919)	1972	Silhouette drawings, comical, tender and full of character. 110 pages with silhouettes on every page.

Copyright © 1990, Good Apple, Inc.

GA1160

Snow White and Rose Red

In a little cottage at the very edge of a deep forest lived a poor widow woman with her two daughters.

The cottage was tiny but did have a patch of garden in which grew two rose trees, one white and the other red. And the widow, who loved her roses, named her daughters after them. She called them Snow White and Rose Red.

Snow White and Rose Red grew up in a gentle, loving way—always kind and thoughtful to their mother and each other.

In the summer they went into the forest to gather berries and firewood and sometimes to play among the tall green trees. And in the winter, when snow covered the ground, they sat at their mother's feet listening to her stories of long ago.

In this manner, the years passed until one dark winter's night someone knocked on the door.

"Let me go," said Snow White, jumping up. And her mother said, "Perhaps some traveler has lost his way in the snow."

It was no traveler who stood there when Snow White opened the door, but a huge brown bear!

Snow White screamed in fright and quickly tried to shut the door. But the bear called out, "Do not be afraid. I will not harm you. I am cold and hungry and seek only shelter for the night."

"Poor bear!" said the widow, going to the door and opening it wide. "You are white with snow. Do please come inside and make use of our fire."

When Snow White and Rose Red saw that the big bear meant them no harm, they went up to him as he lay before the fire and brushed the snow out of his long hair.

Then the mother brought some honey and the bear lapped it up and seemed content to stay there for the whole night.

Copyright © 1990, Good Apple, Inc.

GA1160

Snow White and Rose Red quickly lost all fear of the bear and they played with him and rolled him over and teased him; and the bear accepted all the teasing and fun with the greatest good nature. But as soon as day dawned, the bear called Snow White from her bed and she got up and opened the door and let him go.

All through the long winter the bear came each night and Snow White and Rose Red grew to love him and looked forward to his visits.

"You are our friend," they told him, over and over again. "We shall always love you."

But when spring came, the bear said, "Now I must go into the forest and guard my treasure from the wicked dwarfs."

"Where are they and why do we never see them?" asked Snow White.

"The dwarfs hide under rocks and in caves," said the bear. "But in winter, when the earth is frozen, they must stay underground. It is only in the summer that they try to steal my treasure."

Snow White and Rose Red were sad to see their friend go, and Snow White said, "Maybe we shall meet you in the forest one day and then we can be together again for a short while."

After the bear had gone and the two girls had tidied up the cottage for their mother, they were free to play in the garden or walk in the forest.

Copyright © 1990, Good Apple, Inc.

GA1160

"Let's go to the forest," said Rose Red. "The bear has left us but the forest is green and the birds are singing. We will never feel sad in the forest."

They had only gone a little way when all at once they saw something jumping up and down in the grass.

"What can it be?" Snow White asked. "It's extremely small. Let's go and see."

When they drew near they saw that it was a dwarf with a creased-up face and sharp eyes. They saw, too, that his long white beard was caught in the crevice of a tree trunk so that he could not pull himself free.

As they stood wondering what they could do to help, the little man looked up.

"Don't just stare!" he screamed. "Can't you see what has happened to me? What a pair of idiots you are. Help me!"

"We are wondering what to do for the best," Rose Red explained. "Your beard is well and truly caught."

"We could always try and pull you free." said Snow White doubtfully, "but it might be painful, you know."

"Stop talking and get on with it," replied the dwarf.

Copyright © 1990, Good Apple, Inc.

GA1160

"Very well," said Rose Red, who had a very kind heart and always wanted to help anyone in trouble. "We'll do our best."

And she took hold of the little man by the waist and began to tug.

"Stop it! Stop it!" yelled the little man after only a moment, "You stupid girl! You are making my head ache."

"I know what to do," said Snow White, and she took out a pair of scissors from her pocket. "If we cut his beard we can set him free."

"Don't you dare touch my beautiful beard!" screamed the dwarf, red in the face with anger.

"Then you will have to stay where you are," replied Rose Red, "For it is your beard that is keeping you a prisoner."

When the dwarf did not answer, Snow White bent over him, and snip, snip she cut his beard.

"There you are," she said, beginning to smile. "You have only lost a tiny bit of your beard and you are free."

But before she had finished speaking, the little man was hopping up and down with rage.

"Fool!" he screamed at her. "Look what you have done." You have left the best of my beard in that tree trunk."

"My sister has set you free," said Rose Red gently. "But for her you would still be a prisoner."

Copyright © 1990, Good Apple, Inc.

GA1160

"But for her I would still have all my beard," retorted the dwarf nastily. And he stumped away from them.

As they watched, they saw him pick up a sack, which was filled overflowing with gold pieces, and drag it away.

"What a horrid little man," said Snow White. "If there are any more in the forest like him, I won't feel like coming here."

But the next day was so beautiful that their mother suggested they go into the forest again and enjoy the sunshine.

"You could take your fishing rods," she said, "and see if you can catch a fish for dinner."

"At least we won't be going to that part of the forest where we met the dwarf," Rose Red said, as they made their way to the stream.

As they drew near, they saw through the trees what looked like a giant grasshopper struggling in the air.

"Gracious!" Rose Red exclaimed. "Look over there, Snow White! Whatever is it?"

"Let's find out," said Snow White, and together they ran foward.

To their surprise and dismay, they found themselves staring at the dwarf.

"What are you doing?" asked Rose Red, and she tried not to smile, for the little man looked very funny. "Is anything wrong?"

"Fool!" snapped the tiny man, in the angry voice they had come to expect from him. "Use your eyes! Can't you see that what's left of my beautiful white beard is all twisted up with my fishing line. And what's more, there's a beastly fish at the end of it trying to pull me in and drown me."

"So there is!" said Rose Red, peering down into the water. "But how can we help, I wonder?"

"I'll try and pull you free," offered Snow White, and she took hold of the dwarf by the waist and began to pull him toward her. But the dwarf's beard was twisted so firmly around the fishing line that it did not budge an inch.

This time Rose Red got out her scissors. "I'm sorry," she said, "but if you don't want us to leave you here, you will simply have to agree to having your beard cut."

And with that, snip, snip went her scissors, and the dwarf dropped onto the bank.

Copyright © 1990, Good Apple, Inc.

71

GA1160

"You'll get no thanks from me," he cried, as he hopped away from them. "You've spoiled what was left of my beautiful beard and I'll pay you back one fine day."

As they watched, they saw him take a sack of pearls that lay half hidden in the rushes and drag it behind a big stone.

Soon after this, their mother asked them to go to the village to get some things for her. So, once again, Snow White and Rose Red found themselves in the forest.

"I wonder what trouble our dwarf is in today!" Rose Red laughed, as they ran along.

"Don't laugh," said kindhearted Snow White, as they reached the clearing. "Look, there he is and he seems terrified. Why does he keep looking up at the sky?"

As she spoke, something dark and meancing swooped down on the cringing dwarf.

"Quick!" Rose Red cried. "It's an eagle and already it has got its talons into the dwarf's coat. It's going to carry him off!"

They sprang forward and were only just in time to catch hold of the dwarf. Then it became a tug-of-war between themselves and the strong eagle.

"We've won!" Snow White suddenly shouted, as the eagle, growing tired of the game, released its hold and soared away into the sky.

"Clumsy idiots!" muttered the dwarf. "My good red coat is in shreds now!" And without a word of thanks he went over to a sack of precious stones which was lying on the ground and dragged it into a hole in the rocks.

Copyright © 1990, Good Apple, Inc.

72

GA1160

On the way home, Snow White and Rose Red could not resist talking about the dwarf.

"There's the tree trunk where we first saw him!" said Snow White suddenly. "I wonder where he is now?"

They had only taken a few more steps when they got their answer. For there in a clearing was the dwarf himself, and he was peering down at a carpet of rubies and diamonds and pearls spread out on the green grass. The sun on the precious stones made them shine like stars, and the sisters were fascinated.

"How beautiful!" Snow White whispered, taking hold of her sister's hand. "How did the dwarf come by such a treasure?"

Before Rose Red could reply, the little man glanced up and saw them.

"So it's you again!" he shouted, his face turning red with anger. "Spying on me now!"

Snow White and Rose Red shrank back, as the dwarf moved towards them.

"We-we weren't spying," Snow White stammered. "We were on our way home to our cottage."

"Interfering, meddlesome pair!" raged the dwarf, tugging at what was left of his white beard. "You ruin my beautiful beard, and now you would try to steal my treasures."

Before he could go on, however, there came a loud fierce growl from the direction of the trees, and a huge brown bear lumbered into the clearing.

With a scream of fright, the dwarf darted toward a hole in the rocks, but the bear put out his great paw and pinned him to the ground.

"Spare me, Lord Bear!" whimpered the dwarf. "If you eat me I will only be a morsel in your mouth. Eat these girls instead. See how plump they are!"

For an answer, the bear lifed the struggling dwarf high into the air and then dashed him to the ground.

Then he turned to the sisters. "Do not be afraid," he said. Come closer and you will find that I am your old friend, the bear, who came to you all through the long months of winter."

Snow White took a step forward and as she did so the bear's skin fell from him. Instead of a huge brown bear there now stood a tall handsome young man robed like a Prince.

Copyright © 1990, Good Apple, Inc.

GA1160

Copyright © 1990, Good Apple, Inc.

74

GA1160

Smiling, the Prince told the two sisters his story. "Long ago," he said, "while I was hunting in this very forest, I stumbled upon the dwarf's hideout and all the treasure he and his tribe had been looting from our palace. But, alas, I was no match for the evil leader of the dwarfs who now lies dead. He cast a spell on me before I left the forest and changed me into a bear."

"Poor bear!" Snow White cried. "How glad I am we took you in and gave you shelter when the snow was on the ground."

"Only the dwarf's death could break the spell," the Prince continued, "and now that this has come about the power of the dwarfs is destroyed forever, and all their treasure will be restored to me."

"Now that you are a Prince once again," Rose Red said, "you will not want to come to our humble cottage."

"That is not so," said the Prince, and he turned and looked at Snow White whose golden hair glinted in the sunshine.

"Will you come back with us now?" asked Snow White, a pink flush on her cheeks. "It would make us very happy if you would."

"Indeed I will," answered the Prince, taking her hand, "for there is something I would say to your mother."

Laughing and talking, all three made their way back to the cottage where once again the Prince told his story.

Copyright © 1990, Good Apple, Inc.

GA1160

Then he said, "And now, one thing more, I would like to ask for Snow White's hand in marriage, for I love her with all my heart and want her to be my wife."

The widowed mother readily gave her permission, and the Prince took Snow White back with him to his palace where they married the very next day.

Amid all the rejoicing Snow White found time to whisper to her mother and sister that it was her dearest wish they should leave the cottage and come and stay at the palace. And to this, they readily agreed.

And very soon afterward, the Prince's twin brother fell in love with Rose Red and made her his wife.

The two gentle sisters spread happiness all over the palace and throughout the kingdom, but none was happier than their own dear mother.

She found her greatest joy in just sitting at the window of her royal chamber gazing down into the garden at two rose trees—one red and one white— the very same that had once bloomed in her humble cottage garden.

Copyright © 1990, Good Apple, Inc.

GA1160

Snow White   Rose Red

Name as many things as you are able that are as white as snow.	What things are as red as a rose?
_____	_____
_____	_____
_____	_____
_____	_____
_____	_____
_____	_____
_____	_____
_____	_____
_____	_____
_____	_____
_____	_____
_____	_____
_____	_____
_____	_____
_____	_____

Copyright © 1990, Good Apple, Inc.

GA1160

Questions and Activities About the Story of Snow White and Rose Red

KNOWLEDGE

1. How did the two girls get their names?
2. Where did the dwarf hide?
3. Why was the Prince in the form of a bear?
4. What did the bear say when he came to the door?

COMPREHENSION

1. Why did the girls cut the dwarf's beard?
2. Draw a picture of the eagle pulling the dwarf one way and Snow White and Rose Red pulling him the other.
3. Describe the dwarf.
4. Why was the mother so happy when she looked at her rose trees?

APPLICATION

1. How would it feel to be a human imprisoned in a bear's body?
2. How would you extend the story beyond its ending?

ANALYSIS

1. Where do you think the precious jewels came from?
2. Why did the dwarf call the girls a "meddlesome pair"?
3. Why do you think the dwarf was never grateful when the girls helped him?
4. What word best describes the dwarf?

SYNTHESIS

1. Create a story about a carpet made of rubies, diamonds and pearls.
2. How would the story change if the bear had turned into a poor man?

EVALUATION

1. Why did the Prince choose Snow White instead of Rose Red?
2. How would you feel if you had not been chosen?
3. Describe the Prince's brother who married Rose Red.
4. Instead of the dwarf dying to break the spell over the Prince, how else might the story change?

Copyright © 1990, Good Apple, Inc.

78

GA1160

My Own Story

This page can serve as the cover for a story your students will write. Directions for writing the story as well as back cover for the student created story can be found on the next page.

Copyright © 1990, Good Apple, Inc.

79

GA1160

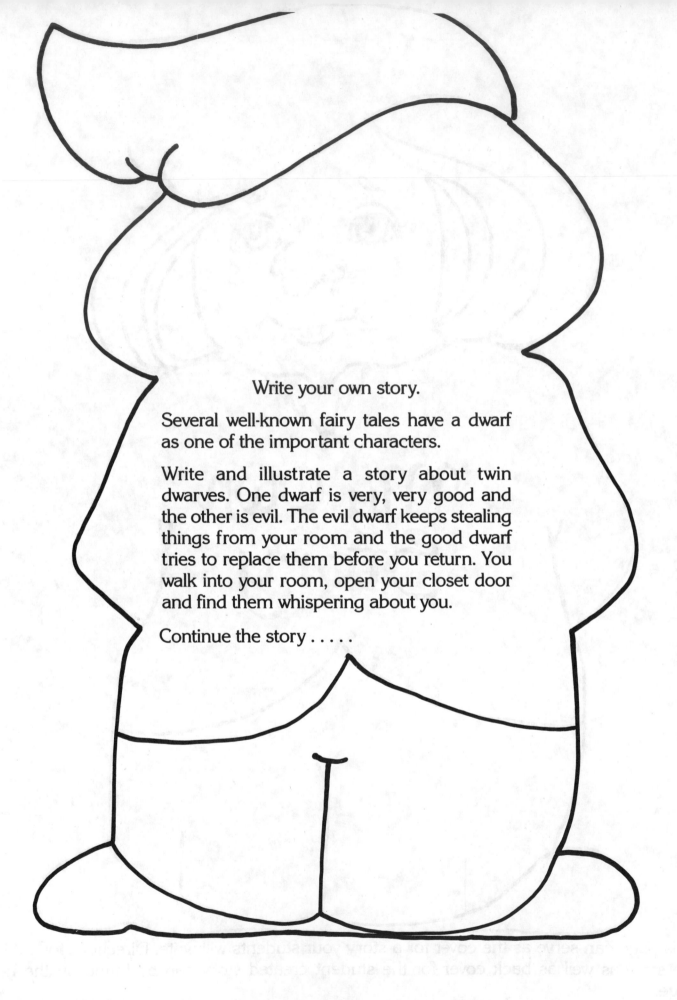

Write your own story.

Several well-known fairy tales have a dwarf as one of the important characters.

Write and illustrate a story about twin dwarves. One dwarf is very, very good and the other is evil. The evil dwarf keeps stealing things from your room and the good dwarf tries to replace them before you return. You walk into your room, open your closet door and find them whispering about you.

Continue the story . . . . .

Copyright © 1990, Good Apple, Inc.

GA1160

Hansel and Gretel

Summary

Once there was a poor woodcutter who lived in the forest with his wife and his children named Hansel and Gretel. Since they were so poor, the woman suggested they leave the children in the forest so they could not find their way home again. Although the thought saddened the father, he could think of no other solution.

On the way into the forest, Hansel dropped sparkled flintstones along the way. They were left there and fell asleep. When the moon came out it shone on the stones and they followed them home.

The mother was not happy to see them and called them "naughty" for getting lost. The next morning she gave them a crust of bread and brought them back into the woods. She told them to wait while she chopped wood. Hansel had dropped bread crumbs along the way, but the tiny birds had eaten them and they had no way of knowing the direction home. They were sad and frightened. Hansel said, "God will take care of us."

In the morning they followed a bird which led them to a little house. It was made of bread, roofed with cakes, and the windows were transparent sugar. They began to eat pieces of the house.

The door opened and out came an old woman. She invited them in and was very kind to them. But really she was a wicked witch who lay in wait for children and had built the little house to entice them.

Her eyes were red and she could not see well. She grasped Hansel with her withered hand and shut him up in a little stable. Then she woke Gretel and made her work about the house cooking and cleaning.

Each day she would ask Hansel to stretch out his finger to see if he was getting fat enough to eat. Hansel would hold out a little bone instead and since the witch could not see well, she thought it was his finger—and he was skinny.

Copyright © 1990, Good Apple, Inc.

GA1160

"Dear God, help us," Gretel prayed.

Early in the morning Gretel had to get up to build a fire in the oven. The witch told her to creep in to see if it was hot enough. When Gretel said she didn't know how, the witch got in to show her. Then Gretel gave her a push—the witch howled frightfully.

Gretel then freed Hansel. They found chests of pearls and precious stones and Gretel filled her apron.

They journeyed through the forest until they came to a great piece of water and wondered how they could get across.

A white duck offered to carry each across on its back, one at a time.

The woods became more and more familiar, and at last they found their father's house. He had missed his children so much. His wife was dead now. Gretel opened her apron. Pearls and precious stones scattered all over the room.

They lived together in great joy after that.

Copyright © 1990, Good Apple, Inc.

GA1160

Puppet Projects

1. Let each student choose a favorite character from a tale by the brothers Grimm. The student should then use a puppet pattern from this book or create an original drawing of that character. Patterns should be colored and mounted first on heavy paper and then on a tongue depressor in order to be easily held. Taping the completed puppet to a ruler will also work nicely.

   Students in turn should hold the completed puppet of choice as he/she tells classmates about the puppet.

   a. Why this character was determined to be the favorite.
   b. What role this character played in the story.
   c. One specific incident from the story that involved the chosen puppet character.

   Puppet patterns can be found on the following pages in this book:
   The Frog, page 31
   The Princess, page 33
   The Frog as a Prince, page 34
   Ugly Stepsisters, page 58
   The Bear, page 68
   Snow White, Rose Red, page 74
   Hansel and Gretel, pages 84-86
   Sleeping Beauty, pages 89-90
   Spinning Fairies, page 104
   Fisherman's Wife, page 110
   Rapunzel's Mother, page 37
   Rapunzel, page 42
   Cinderella, pages 48, 55, 56
   The Prince, page 49
   The Dwarf, page 72
   The Prince, page 75
   The Witch, page 87
   Little Red Riding Hood, page 97
   The Fisherman, page 109

2. Creative movement time can be more fun by using student-made stick puppets. As music from *The Magic Flute* is played, students can move about the classroom as they hold stick puppets. Pretending to be a famous fairy tale character can ease inhibition.

3. Have each student create a stick puppet. When completed, place all puppets in a pile. At random draw four or five of the puppets from the pile. Have students claim puppets. A group has been formed. The task for the group is to write a fairy tale that involves the puppets.

Copyright © 1990, Good Apple, Inc.

GA1160

Copyright © 1990, Good Apple, Inc.

GA1160

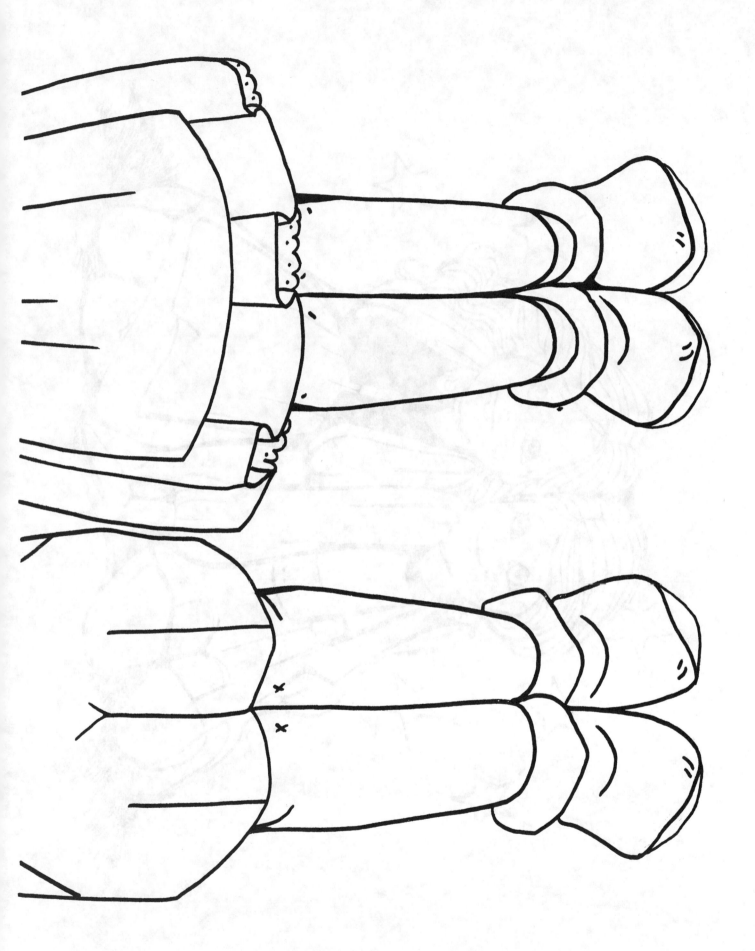

Copyright © 1990, Good Apple, Inc.

85

GA1160

Copyright © 1990, Good Apple, Inc.

86

GA1160

Copyright © 1990, Good Apple, Inc.

87

GA1160

How many stories can you name that have a

Prince

_____

_____

_____

_____

_____

How many can you name that have a

Witch

_____

_____

_____

_____

_____

_____

How many have a

King and Queen

_____

_____

_____

_____

_____

Copyright © 1990, Good Apple, Inc.

Sleeping Beauty

Summary

A fish bestows the blessing of a child on a childless queen for her kindness. When a baby princess is born, all the good fairies are invited and present wonderful gifts to the child. One fairy is not invited because there isn't enough room, but she appears anyway and puts an evil spell on the baby. "She will prick her finger on a spindle and die"; then she leaves.

One little fairy hasn't given her gift yet, so she says. Although she cannot take away the evil fairy's wish, she can change it. "She will not die, but she will sleep for 100 years."

The king decreed that all spindles be banned from the kingdom.

When the princess is fifteen, she wanders into a very old part of the castle where an old woman is spinning. The woman had never heard the king's decree. The princess asks to see the spindle, pricks her finger and the whole kingdom falls asleep for 100 years.

Just as the hundred years are up, a handsome prince hears about the beautiful princess, cuts his way through the thorn bushes, finds her and kisses her. The whole kingdom slowly awakes. All the activity resumes and the princess and the prince are married.

Copyright © 1990, Good Apple, Inc.

GA1160

Copyright © 1990, Good Apple, Inc.

The Royal Baker is falling asleep under the witch's spell. Draw the things that might happen in his kitchen if he fell asleep while cooking.

Copyright © 1990, Good Apple, Inc.

91

GA1160

Sleeping Beauty's Wedding Cake

The layers of the wedding cake have been numbered for you. On the reverse side of this sheet, tell about the flavor and ingredients for each layer. Layer three, for example, could be a strawberry and banana cream delight. Then use your imagination to decorate each layer.

Copyright © 1990, Good Apple, Inc.

92

GA1160

A Crayon Resist Sleeping Beauty

You will need:

> drawing paper
> thin black tempera paint
> crayons
> wide paintbrush
> newspaper

Draw a scene from the story of Sleeping Beauty in crayon.

It is important that your crayoned areas be covered with a thick layer of crayon. Dark crayons won't show up well. If you want an area to remain white, you'll need to color it with a white crayon.

Put your drawing on newspaper. Lightly brush one coat of paint over the whole picture.

You will notice that the wax crayon repels the paint and shows through.

Copyright © 1990, Good Apple, Inc.

GA1160

Questions on Sleeping Beauty

KNOWLEDGE
1. Who are the main characters in the story?
2. How did the princess fall asleep?
3. Which fairy cast the sleeping spell?

COMPREHENSION
1. Why did the evil fairy cast a death spell?
2. Give an example of a kindness extended in the story.
3. Why did the king banish spinning wheels?

APPLICATION
1. If the evil spell would not have been placed on the princess, what might have happened in the story?
2. Illustrate the kingdom before the prince awakened the princess with a kiss.
3. Interview the evil fairy to find out why she cursed the princess and how she felt when another lessened the curse.

ANALYSIS
1. Did the princess have any control over what was happening in her life?
2. How would the countryside and environment have changed over 100 years?
3. What is similar in the story of Snow White and that of Sleeping Beauty?
4. Explain how the old woman would not have heard of the king's decree banning spinning wheels.

SYNTHESIS
1. Role-play the town coming awake after 100 years.
2. How did the sleeping kingdom affect trade with other countries?
3. If you had been the king, how would you have protected your daughter?
4. If you were the last fairy to grant a wish, what would you have said?

EVALUATION
1. What does *happily ever after* mean?
2. How would you write the end to this story?
3. How could the entire situation have been avoided?
4. How would the townspeople act toward the evil fairy after awakening?

Copyright © 1990, Good Apple, Inc.

GA1160

Little Red Riding Hood

Summary

Once a sweet little girl was loved so much by her grandmother that Granny made her a cap of red velvet and the child never went without it, so everyone called her Little Red Riding Hood.

One day she was taking a basket of cakes to her grandmother. She had to travel through the woods and there she met a wolf. He asked where she was going, and she said she was taking cakes to her grandmother who lived across the forest. The wolf thought the little girl would be very tender to eat, so he hurried away to the grandmother's house and pretended he was the little girl. When the grandmother let him in, he gobbled her up, put on her bonnet and got in her bed. When Little Red Riding Hood arrived, she noticed her grandmother looked a little different and said what large ears and eyes she had.

Then she said what a terrible large mouth she had. The wolf jumped out of bed and ate the child.

A woodsman was walking by the house and heard the wolf snoring after he had fallen asleep. Something was moving in his stomach so the woodsman took a shears and snipped at the wolf's body. Out popped Grandmother and Red Riding Hood unharmed.

They put stones in his stomach and sewed him up as he slept. When he woke up and went for a drink in the river, he was so heavy he drowned.

When another wolf tried the same trick and wanted to eat the grandmother and child, they tricked him instead. Then Little Red Riding Hood went home unharmed.

Copyright © 1990, Good Apple, Inc.

GA1160

Word Search

Find these words from the story of Little Red Riding Hood.

grandmother	forest	cap
huntsman	teeth	woods
Red Riding Hood	latch	Grimm
wolf	door	tale
mouth	gobbled	granddaughter
basket	stones	trees
tail	cut	path
eat	frightened	visit
ears		

```
R  S  R  E  T  H  G  U  A  D  D  N  A  R  G
S  P  F  O  N  T  I  S  I  V  Z  D  O  O  R
R  W  O  L  F  A  V  W  X  Y  A  B  C  E  A
A  C  R  X  M  P  B  H  U  N  T  S  M  A  N
E  A  E  S  K  L  I  C  G  O  B  B  L  E  D
V  P  S  J  T  G  H  D  R  F  J  K  D  R  M
F  G  T  I  A  F  E  G  I  R  K  I  N  P  O
W  L  T  E  E  T  H  I  M  I  L  D  C  U  T
X  H  K  J  Y  E  T  F  M  G  S  S  P  S  H
Q  W  O  O  D  S  U  M  O  H  L  I  A  T  E
O  P  M  N  Z  L  O  N  P  T  H  S  B  O  R
E  U  T  S  R  A  M  Q  H  E  O  D  C  N  I
B  A  S  K  E  T  Z  L  O  N  O  C  D  E  N
T  R  E  E  S  C  T  A  L  E  N  A  B  S  L
R  I  D  O  O  H  G  N  I  D  I  R  D  E  R
```

Copyright © 1990, Good Apple, Inc.

GA1160

Copyright © 1990, Good Apple, Inc.

97

GA1160

Help Little Red Riding Hood
find her way to Granny's.

GRANNY

Copyright © 1990, Good Apple, Inc.

98

GA1160

Goodies for Grandmother

Little Red Riding Hood had filled a basket full of goodies to take to her grandmother. Little Red was so busy she did not have time to spell the names of the goodies correctly. That will have to be your job. Unscramble each word and place it in the correctly numbered section of the basket.

1. p e s p l a
2. c c s u e k p a
3. e c e s h e
4. c s r r a e c k
5. d a y c n
6. o k s e i o c

7. n s o e r g a
8. t e p u a n t r e b u t
9. z a p i z
10. k n e c i h c
11. s e e p a h c
12. a s n a a b n

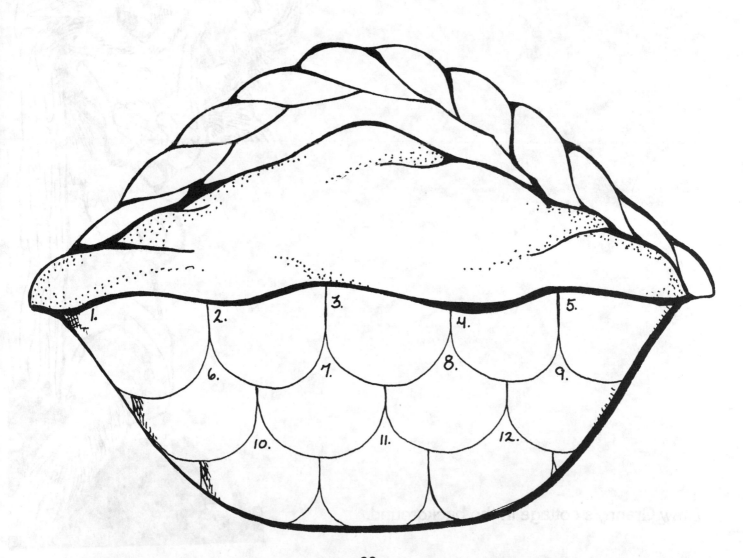

Copyright © 1990, Good Apple, Inc.

99

GA1160

Draw Granny's cottage in the background.

Copyright © 1990, Good Apple, Inc.

GA1160

Job Application Form

(For a prince, princess, witch, king, queen, wolf, etc.)

Name _____ Date _____

         (Last)   (First)   (Middle)

Birth Date ____ / ____ / ____ Social Security Number _____

Address _____

      Street   City   State   Zip

Phone (____) _____ Marital Status _____

     Area Code

Briefly state your career goals.

_____

_____

State your qualifications.

_____

_____

Previous related work experience:

Job Title	Dates (From / To)	Responsibilities
1.		
2.		
3.		
4.		

How would this job make a difference in your life?

_____

_____

_____

Copyright © 1990, Good Apple, Inc.

GA1160

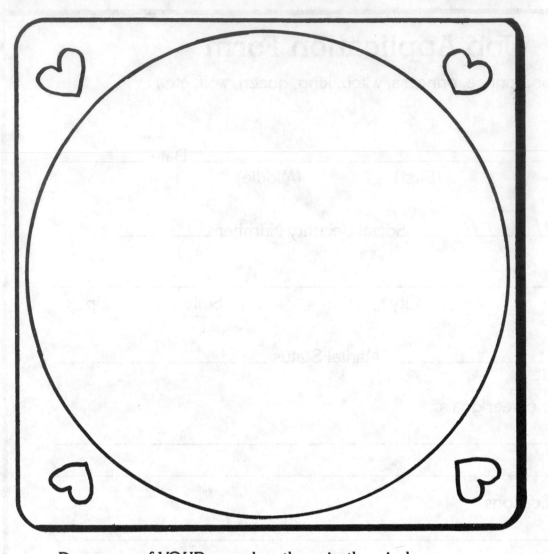

Draw one of YOUR grandmothers in the circle.

List the things you like about her.

_____

_____

_____

_____

_____

_____

_____

_____

_____

_____

Grandmothers

Copyright © 1990, Good Apple, Inc.

102

GA1160

The Three Spinning Fairies

Summary

Once there was a lazy girl who hated to work and would not help her mother spin. The mother was so ashamed of her she told all her friends that the girl loved to spin. The queen was passing by and heard the rumor. She asked to take the girl with her because she loved the sound of spinning. The queen promised the girl that if she could spin all the flax, she would marry her oldest son. As soon as the queen left the room, the girl began to cry. In her weeping she looked out the window and saw three funny looking women. One had a big, flat foot; another a large under lip that hung over her chin, and the third a very broad thumb.

They offered to spin for the girl if she would introduce them as her cousins and not be ashamed of them. "This I will gladly promise," said the girl.

The three women began to spin and did not stop unti the flax in three rooms had been spun. And so the wedding took place. In walked the three women attired in the most wonderful dresses. The bridegroom could not understand why they were so ugly. The first explained that she had such a broad foot from turning the spinning wheel, the second said her lip was so large from moistening the thread and the third told that her thumb was so broad from twisting the thread.

"Then," cried the prince, "my beautiful wife shall never go near a spinning wheel again as long as she lives."

And so she was rid of the hated task of spinning forever.

Copyright © 1990, Good Apple, Inc.

GA1160

Copyright © 1990, Good Apple, Inc.

104

GA1160

Fairies

The word *fairy* appears in many stories and can have several different meanings. Usually a fairy is referred to as a little imaginary person. People believed in fairies for hundreds of years, even before books were being printed. Most fairy tales refer to these little people in one way or another, and the belief in them was strongest during the Middle Ages. Fairy characteristics altered slightly from one country to another but most have several in common.

Common to most were these characteristics:

were immortal or lived a very long time

had magical powers

could appear and disappear at will

could cast spells and change shape

could marry and have children

A comparison of these imaginary creatures is charted on the following pages, but for more information and detailed descriptions, check the *World Book Encyclopedia* under the subject of "Fairies," 1988 Edition, Vol. 7, pages 10-11.

Copyright © 1990, Good Apple, Inc.

GA1160

Classification of Fairies

Name for Fairy	Country	Description of Characteristics
Fee	Germany and France	Were immortal or lived long, had magical powers, could appear and disappear, cast spells and change shape, could marry and have children
Fata	Italy	
Hada	Spain	
Vila	Slavic	White fairy who decides destiny of newborn infants
Hsien	China	Wise mountain man or elf who was immortal
Flower Fairy	Japan	Loved to dance and enjoy music
Noble Fairies	Brittany and England	Invisible creatures from the royal court of Fairyland. They lived in a palace and had a fairy army. They liked to dance in rings and had lords and ladies. Their king was Oberon and the queen was Titania.
Household Fairies		
Elves	Scandinavia	Were good or evil. The good ones lived in the air and the bad lived underground.
Goblins	France	They came unexpectedly and were mean. They lived in houses and pinched naughty children.
Kobolds	Germany	They lived in mines underground. They could be cheerful or start quarrels among people. They liked to clean houses.
Leprechauns	Ireland	They made shoes for the fairies. They looked like little old men and no one was to believe what they said.
Nixes	Germany	They lived in lakes and rivers and led people to dangerous waters. They looked half human but had fish tails.
Pixies	England	People believed these were the souls of babies who died before they had been baptized. They lived in the rocks.
Poltergeists	Germany	Noisy ghosts
Trolls	Scandinavia	Trolls did not like noise. They were short, ugly men with humped backs. They did not want to harm people and usually lived in caves.

Copyright © 1990, Good Apple, Inc.

GA1160

Papier-Mâché Masks

Materials needed:

paper towels torn in strips
water
wheat or wallpaper paste
bowl

one balloon for each child
paint
yarn, egg cartons, etc.

1. Mix one cup of paste to ten (10) cups of warm water.

2. Blow up balloons.

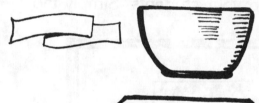

3. Dip paper towel strips into paste and put on in layers on half of the balloon.

4. Make the nose, ears, etc., stick out. You may want to add pieces of egg carton and put wet strips over those parts.

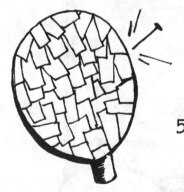

5. Use at least three layers.

6. After it is hard and dry, pop the balloon and paint the mask. You can add yarn hair or hats if you like.

7. Display throughout the classroom.

Copyright © 1990, Good Apple, Inc.

GA1160

Tell a Story in Costume

A blonde wig, a red cape, a prissy little dress and a large basket of freshly baked cookies is all that is needed to make the telling of "Little Red Riding Hood" a very special occasion.

Enter the classroom on your chosen day, maybe just after recess, in costume. Go to a chair and tell the students your version of "Little Red Riding Hood" or another brothers Grimm tale of your choosing.

What special motivation this simple costume will provide. And, of course, when the telling of the tale is completed, each child will receive a freshly baked cookie.

Cinderella

An old prom or bridesmaid's dress and fancy slippers could turn you into an instant fairy godmother. Add a tiara or crown of gold foil and a magic wand made from a wrapping paper tube. After telling the story of "Cinderella" it will be in your power to grant a special wish to your students. Simply tap each gently with the wand.

Copyright © 1990, Good Apple, Inc.

GA1160

The Fisherman and His Wife

Summary

A poor fisherman, out to catch the day's meal, caught a large flounder at the end of his line. This was a magical fish and asked to be set free. The kindhearted fisherman returned him to the sea and then left empty-handed to return to his wife in their poor hovel. When he told his wife of the fish, she called him a fool and said he should have asked the fish to grant a wish in exchange for his life. She forced him to return to the sea and call the fish forth.

"My wife wishes us to have a little cottage," cried the man to the fish. "So be it," said the fish and when the man returned, a fine cottage awaited him. With each day the wife became more greedy. She wished for a stone castle with maids and servants. The fish granted the wish. Again she became dissatisfied. "I will be king," she said. It was granted.

Weeks passed. "I will be emperor," was her next demand.

Again the wish was granted. Several days went by and now she insisted on becoming Pope. She did so.

At last she demanded, "I will be lord of the universe."

With that, in a whirlwind they were both returned to the poor hovel where they had begun.

As far as we know they are still there.

Copyright © 1990, Good Apple, Inc.

GA1160

Copyright © 1990, Good Apple, Inc.

110

GA1160

Writing Activities

Animals in Fairy Tales

On this page and the next you will find several writing activities. Choose two of them to work on independently.

1. Write a fairy tale which involves your favorite animal, a magician and a beautiful young girl.

2. Write a fairy tale about three animals who become friends and create their own kingdom. Who becomes the ruler? Where is this kingdom? What is it like there?

3. In the story "The Fisherman and His Wife," a magic fish plays an important role. In many other fairy tales other animals play important roles. How many can you think of? Each animal must be different.

Animal	Tale
_____	_____
_____	_____
_____	_____
_____	_____
_____	_____
_____	_____
_____	_____

4. Take a human character from one fairy tale, perhaps Snow White, and an animal from another fairy tale, perhaps the wolf from "Little Red Riding Hood." Weave an original fairy tale based on this new character grouping.

Copyright © 1990, Good Apple, Inc.

GA1160

5. Choose one of the titles listed below. Write a one-page summary of a fairy tale with that title.

> The Fisherman and the Golden Goose
> Snow White, Cinderella and the Wolf
> The Golden Goose and the Cobbler
> The Elves and the Frog Prince
> Three Spinning Fairies and the Cobbler
> Sleeping Beauty and the Fisherman

6. Create a telephone book. First make a list of characters in the fairy tales of the brothers Grimm. Then look how people are listed in your community's telephone book. Now you are ready to create your Fairy Tale Phone Book. Be sure to include some animals.

7. Today Clark Kent changes into Superman or Bruce Wayne becomes Batman. This is really a modern version of a fairy tale happening. The bear becomes Prince Charming, for example. Choose a fairy tale by the brothers Grimm. Rewrite it as if it happened in the 1990's.

8. Many times an animal in a fairy tale has no name. The animal is simply referred to as the goose, the frog, the wolf or the bear. Choose one animal. Give him/her a name, an address as well as personality and background. For example:

> Wanda A. Wolf lives in Growley, Colorado. One of her neighbors, Grandma Hood, describes her as a hardworking lady who roams the forests of the area. The elderly Mrs. Hood, however, is quick to mention that in winter when food is scarce Wanda can often be found hiding behind a tree waiting to snatch morsels of food from unsuspecting passersby.
>
> Wanda has never married and has no means of support except for . . . .

9. It seems that some animals are never mentioned in fairy tales. A tiger or a giraffe would be examples. Why are these animals seldom, if ever, mentioned?

Let's not neglect these animal friends. Choose an animal like a hippopotamus or a kangaroo and write a fairy tale involving that animal. Just think of the possibilities. "Sleeping Beauty Goes to Australia" (a kangaroo).

Copyright © 1990, Good Apple, Inc.

GA1160

The Golden Goose

Summary

Once there lived a man who had three sons. The youngest son was called Dummling. When wood for the fire had to be cut, the eldest son went into the woods to chop a tree. As he was working, a little old man bid him good day and asked for something to eat. "The food I have is for me alone," said the son. With that he missed a stroke of the ax and cut himself. He had to return home to care for the injury.

The second son went to complete the work. Again the little old man appeared and asked for food. "If you eat, there will not be as much for me," said the boy. He aimed at the tree but hit his leg instead. Then he, too, returned home. Dummling set out to try his hand at cutting wood. When the little old man appeared to him, he was happy to share the little food he had. As a reward the man told him to cut down a certain tree and he would find something wonderful at the root. When he had finished chopping the tree, Dummling found a goose with feathers of pure gold at its roots. He took the goose and went to spend the night at a nearby inn.

The innkeeper had three daughters who wanted a pure gold feather for themselves. As the first touched the goose, she stuck fast and could not pull away. As the second tried to help her, she took the first girl's hand and stuck to her. Seeing their distress, the third came to help and as luck would have it, she stuck, too. The parson saw the situation and ran to their aid. As he touched the third daughter he also stuck fast. Next, a clerk and two laborers tried to help, and you can guess what happened to them. Along came Dummling and picked up his goose with the seven following in tow. He wanted to see the world. They came to a city where the king had a daughter who never laughed. The king had promised her to any man who could get a laugh out of her. She looked out the window and as soon as she saw the seven all attached to the goose, she let out a loud, loud laugh. Then Dummling claimed her for his wife and he became heir to the throne.

What became of the goose was never heard.

Copyright © 1990, Good Apple, Inc.

113

GA1160

Copyright © 1990, Good Apple, Inc.

114

GA1160

Fairy Tale Topics

On this page you will find some possibilities, some ideas, some suggestions. Choose one of them. Create a fairy tale in your mind. No writing is necessary. Just imaginative thinking. Draw a picture relating to the fairy tale you create and show it to your classmates while you tell them the tale you have created.

1. Pretend that Snow White and Rose Red have a third sister. What is her name? What is she like? Is she good or evil? Is she younger or older? Retell this fairy tale but be sure to include the new character.

2. The telephone has just been invented. Cinderella calls her fairy godmother. What do they say? Why did Cinderella make the call. Maybe the fairy godmother returns Cinderella's call. Maybe not. What if one of the mean stepsisters answered the return call? Does either Cinderella or the fairy godmother have an answering machine? If so, what is the message?

3. You are the main character in a fairy tale. You are given a china pig covered with rubies. Why? What happens? Somehow a live pig must be involved in the fairy tale you create.

4. After shoving the wicked witch into the oven, a panting and frightened Gretel stumbles to the door of the cottage. She knows she has committed murder. Continue the story.

5. The fisherman has never married but still he catches the magic fish. Tell about this twist of events in the story. What would the fisherman want and what would happen?

6. You have been given a magic cat whose meow is the most beautiful music in the world. A famous musician wants the cat to sing and perform for the king. The musician offers to buy your cat for all the money in the world but you have grown very fond of this lovable animal. What happens? What do you do? What does the musician do? Is a magic spell cast?

7. You are a beautiful young princess or a handsome prince. One morning you awake and find that your hair has grown to be over twenty feet long. When you try to cut it, it grows back faster and longer. It gets in your way. You are fired from your job. You trip and fall over it. What happens?

Copyright © 1990, Good Apple, Inc.

GA1160

What the Goose Started You Must Finish

It is your task to color these special eggs that the goose has laid. One egg should be golden. As you color these truly beautiful eggs, think about what special things could fit inside an egg. When you are finished, your teacher will give you an egg to take home. Bring this egg back tomorrow with something special hidden inside. You will give clues, and your classmates will try to guess what's inside.

Copyright © 1990, Good Apple, Inc.

116

GA1160

Note to Teacher: Use the plastic eggs found at Eastertime.

The Elves and the Cobbler

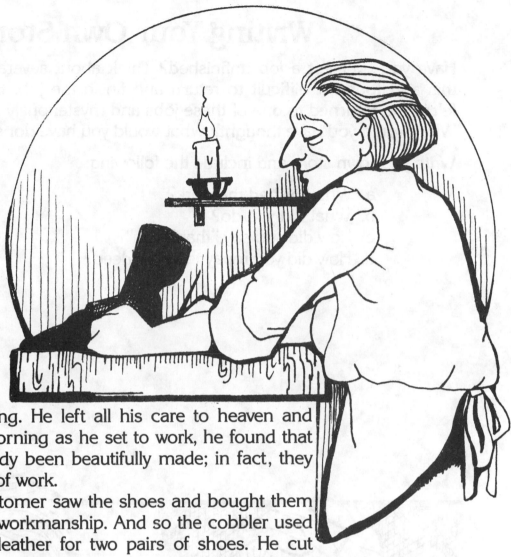

Summary

Once there was an honest cobbler who was poor, although he worked very hard. Finally he had only enough leather left to make one pair of shoes.

He cut out the leather and went to bed thinking he would finish the shoes in the morning. He left all his care to heaven and fell asleep. In the morning as he set to work, he found that the shoes had already been beautifully made; in fact, they were a masterpiece of work.

Later that day a customer saw the shoes and bought them because of the fine workmanship. And so the cobbler used the money to buy leather for two pairs of shoes. He cut the leather and went to bed.

In the morning the work was done as before, every stitch a beauty. He then bought leather for four pairs of shoes, cut it and went to bed. Again as before he found the beautiful shoes waiting for him.

Finally he and his wife decided to hide and watch for the one who did this marvelous work. At midnight, two little naked dwarfs appeared. They began to stitch, rap and tap until the work was finished. Then they left as quick as lightning.

"They have nothing on their backs to keep the cold away," said the wife. "I will make them each a shirt and coat, a waistcoat and pantaloons." "And I will make them little shoes," said the cobbler. And they set to work. When the work was quite finished, they laid the things on the table and hid. About midnight the dwarfs came in dancing and skipping. When they saw the clothes and shoes they were delighted. They put them on and danced, capered and sprang about. They danced out the window never to return. The good couple saw them no more, but everything went well for them and they were happy as long as they lived.

Copyright © 1990, Good Apple, Inc.

GA1160

Writing Your Own Story

Have you ever left a job unfinished? Think about several times that you did this and found it difficult to return and finish the job. How would you have felt if you returned to one of these jobs and mysteriously it had been finished? What would you have thought? What would you have done?

Write your own story and include the following:

        a. Who finished the work?
        b. What did you do?
        c. How did you say "thank you"?
        d. How did you repay the kind deed?

Copyright © 1990, Good Apple, Inc.

GA1160

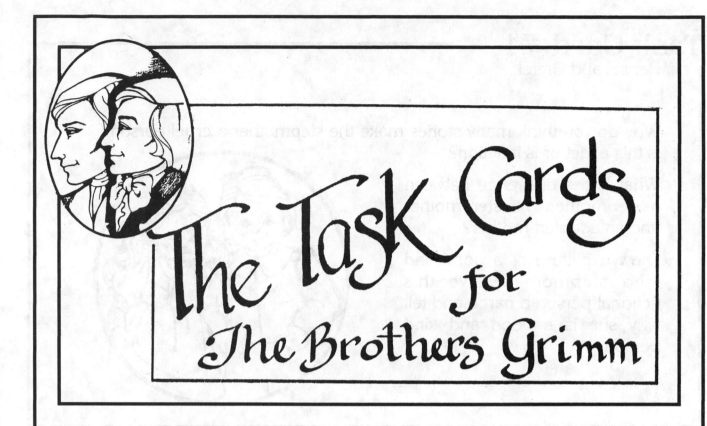

The Task Cards for The Brothers Grimm

Thoughts to the teacher:

1. The task cards on the following pages may be used for individualized project work or as assignments for the entire class. Many of the questions presented can simply be used as motivators for class discussions.

2. It is suggested that the task cards be cut apart. Each could then be mounted on a piece of construction paper or tagboard, laminated and placed in the learning center. A hole could be punched in the upper right corner of each card and they could be loosely bound with a metal ring.

3. Each card could be colored and glued to the front of a manila folder. The task folders could be placed in a cardboard box and students could place completed work in appropriate folders.

4. You may choose to duplicate the task cards so that each student in your classroom could have his/her own set. A contract form could be duplicated and each student could determine (with your guidance) what work would be completed within a set period of time.

Copyright © 1990, Good Apple, Inc.

GA1160

Task Card #1
Hansel and Gretel

Why do you think many stories make the stepmother a cruel person? Is this a fact or is it fiction?

What is the difference between a stepmother, a foster mother and an adopted mother?

Draw a picture of a good and kind stepmother. Give this fictional person a name and tell why she is a good and kind person.

Task Card #2
The Frog Prince

Use construction paper, scissors, some markers and glue and make a crown for the Prince. On the crown should be a picture of a frog to remind the Prince of what he once was.

Copyright © 1990, Good Apple, Inc.

GA1160

Task Card #3

Cinderella

Create a new version of the story of Cinderella. In this new version, Cinderella is not neglected or treated cruelly. She is beautiful and has a wonderful life. However the stepsisters are mistreated by their mother. They are forced to work and wear rags.

Task Card #4

Little Red Riding Hood

You are excited. Next Saturday you are going to visit your grandmother. Your grandmother, just like Little Red Riding Hood's grandmother, is not feeling well. She is not really sick; she is just not feeling well. What things would you take to your grandmother? Plan what the two of you will do together. How will you spend the day?

Copyright © 1990, Good Apple, Inc.

GA1160

Task Card #5

Rapunzel

You know you are going to be locked in a tower. You will be there for one month. You will not be able to leave. What will you take with you? You are limited to just eight things.

or

Draw a diagram of your tower cell. Show where everything is located.

Task Card #6

Sleeping Beauty

Pretend you are Sleeping Beauty. You have been asleep for 100 years. Make a list of what has changed when you awake.

or

Talk to an elderly person that you know. This person should be at least seventy years old. Ask this person to help you make a list. The list should be things that we have today that did not exist when that person was a child.

Copyright © 1990, Good Apple, Inc.

GA1160

Task Card #7

The Fisherman and His Wife

Would you have been satisfied after having the fish grant one wish?

Make a list of reasons why the fisherman's wife was never happy.

Draw her as emperoress.

Task Card #8

The Three Spinning Fairies

Do you think the girl in the fairy tale deserved to marry the Prince since she led him to believe that she had spun all the straw when she actually did no work at all? Why? Why not?

or

Write a different ending to the story.

Copyright © 1990, Good Apple, Inc.

GA1160

Task Card #9

The Golden Goose

Write and illustrate a short story telling what happened to the goose with the feathers of pure gold. Your story should begin just after the wedding of Dummling and the Princess. It should take place during the time they ruled the kingdom.

Task Card #10

Snow White and Rose Red

Choose one of the characters listed below and tell why you would like to have been this character in the story. It is your choice; you can be:

Snow White   The Prince   Rose Red   The Bear

Copyright © 1990, Good Apple, Inc.

GA1160

Task Card #11

1. In what ways are fairy tales different from real life stories? Make a list.

2. What kind of characters can be found in fairy tales that cannot be found in real life?

3. What is your favorite fairy tale? Briefly tell why it is your favorite.

Task Card #12

It is true. You have a good fairy of your very own. She will be with you for one entire year.

What would you name your fairy?

What would you have your fairy do for you?

Do you have any kind of obligation to the fairy? Why? What obligation?

Copyright © 1990, Good Apple, Inc.

GA1160

Task Card #13

The Elves and the Cobbler

What would you like the elves to finish for you?

Draw a picture of you and the elves finishing that task.

Task Card #14

1. Choose your favorite character from a brothers Grimm fairy tale. Tell why this is your favorite character.

2. Today we have science fiction stories like *Star Trek*. How are these modern stories alike and different from the tales of the brothers Grimm?

3. Choose a story by the brothers Grimm and rewrite it and make it modern, more like the stories we have today. Would the Prince's name be Rocky? Would Indiana Jones be disguised in a bear's skin?

Copyright © 1990, Good Apple, Inc.

GA1160

Extending the Lesson

Social Studies

1. A little geographical information is given in each of the stories by the brothers Grimm. The animals, the plants, the terrain described give some clues. List these geographical clues for each story and then try to determine which country in Europe or which state in America is similar to the setting of the story.

2. On an outline map locate each of these countries or states.

3. Pretend that the story of Cinderella had taken place in the desert. Retell the story leaving no doubt about the geographical area.

4. Kings, queens, princes and princesses exist today. Great Britain has Prince Charles, Queen Elizabeth and Princess Diana. America does not. What is the government like in a nation that has kings and queens? How is it different from the government we have in America?

Mathematics

1. Sleeping Beauty slept for 100 years. How many days, hours, months and weeks was that?

2. Many people sleep eight hours a night. If you do that and live to be seventy-five years old, how many hours would you sleep? How many days, weeks, months and years is that?

3. Cinderella had to leave the ball at the stroke of midnight. On a twenty-four-hour clock that is 24:00. How is a twenty-four-hour clock different from the way we tell time? Practice telling time using the twenty-four-hour clock method. Where is this type of time reporting used? Why? Create some addition and subtraction of time problems using this method.

4. Create some story problems based on the happenings in each of the tales by the brothers Grimm.

Science

1. Time ages everyone. Try to find several pictures of yourself, one as a baby and one for each two years of your life. Arrange them in order and study them. As you have aged, what changes have taken place?

   Ask an older person to gather pictures of himself/herself at various ages. Compare these photographs. Draw some conclusions.

   Enlarge a black and white photograph of yourself on a copying machine. Use a pencil and your imagination and try to age yourself. What do you think you will look like at the age of seventy?

2. Some things in nature are almost as magic as occurrences in fairy tales. In autumn when the leaves on the trees turn red, orange and yellow, it is as if someone has waved a magic wand.

Copyright © 1990, Good Apple, Inc.

GA1160

However, in science these happenings are scientific, not magical. What is the scientific explanation for the changing of the color of a tree's leaves?

List several almost magical happenings of science and then try to discover the scientific explanation.

In science the change of a tadpole into a frog is almost as magical as the frog changing into a prince in the story.

3. In the tale of "Snow White and Rose Red," the Prince was simply covered with the skin of a bear. Some hunters today kill a bear and make a rug. Do some research and learn about the process of tanning. The science of taxidermy is also used today as a means of preserving something. Learn more about taxidermy.

Language Arts

1. Write a poem that might break the spell and change the frog back into the prince.

2. In the language style used in the telling of fairy tales, sometimes different words or phrases are used.

   When they drew near . . . .

   We are wondering what to do for the best . . . .

   . . . she longed for it thrice . . . .

   are three examples. Clarify the meanings of the phrases. Find at least ten more examples from the fairy tales of the brothers Grimm. After each example on your list, give a translation.

3. Create a new fairy tale using characters from more than one story.

   Cinderella and the Wolf

   Little Red Riding Hood and the Elves

4. Make a list of smaller words that you can spell from the letters c-i-n-d-e-r-e-l-l-a. Alphabetize your list.

   After the individual lists are made and alphabetized, group the students four or five to a group. Each group should make a master group. Finally, a composite class list should be made.

   Allow time for each group to use a dictionary and try to find additional words to place on the class list.

   Even the best speller is bound to learn a couple of new words.

Physical Education

Have a Brothers Grimm Olympics. A Frog Prince hoping race, a Rapunzel rope climb, a Snow White and Rose Red three-legged race, an all fours bear race, a Little Red Skipping Hood race, and an Elves and the Cobbler shoe-lacing race are just a few suggestions.

Copyright © 1990, Good Apple, Inc.

GA1160

The Learning Center

The purpose of the learning center is to help develop independent learning in an exciting and meaningful way. It should be an area in the classroom where specific learning can take place. The center helps children learn at their own pace.

It provides opportunities for different ways of learning and an integration of many curricular areas.

A sample learning center has been set up on the following page. All the activities and task cards are found in this book.

This center may include:

activities	construction and paint center
work sheets	task cards
puppets	drama
listening center	record keeping

The materials needed are

handouts of the activities	glue
work sheets	construction paper
puppets (one set completed by the teacher)	fabric and yarn
	tape recorder and/or record player
task cards	records or tapes
paintbrushes	headsets
scissors	chairs

How simple or how complicated the learning center you create is should depend on the ages of your students. Another factor to consider is how much exposure your students have had to the learning center approach.

Young learners and first-time learners will enjoy and benefit from a simple learning center. Three or four possible tasks would work well. An elaborate center would be frustrating. Plan for just a few options. More options can be presented the next week. If new activities are added on a regular basis, a learning center can remain inviting for a lengthy period of time.

A special time should be set aside to introduce the learning center to your students. Each activity, each option should be carefully explained. This will save a lot of questions. Remember that many times it is insecurity that causes questioning. Students want to do things correctly. Establish rules and guidelines for use of the learning center.

You, the teacher, know best what kind of learning center will work in your classroom.

Copyright © 1990, Good Apple, Inc.

GA1160

The Brothers Grimm

Brothers Grimm Learning Center

Display Area

Puppets

Task Cards

Activities

Work Sheets

Scissors

Fabric - Yarn

Brushes

Glue

Paint

Colored Paper

Records

Tapes

Copyright © 1990, Good Apple, Inc.

130

Learning Center Record Keeping

List of Activities

Names

Copyright © 1990, Good Apple, Inc.

GA1160

Learning Center Contract

I, _____, agree to complete the

                student's name (printed)

following projects/activities/work sheets by _____

                                                        date

1. _____

    _____

2. _____

    _____

3. _____

    _____

4. _____

    _____

5. _____

    _____

I know the rules for using the learning center and will abide by them. I will also try to do my very best job.

_____

        student's signature

_____ efforts will be evaluated by the follow-

        student's name (printed)

ing terms and conditions: _____

_____

_____

                             _____

                                     teacher's signature

                             _____

                                     student's signature

Copyright © 1990, Good Apple, Inc.

GA1160

Tales from the Brothers Grimm

The Bearskinner, ill. by Felix Hoffmann, Atheneum, 1978.

The Brave Little Tailor, adapted by Audry Claus, ill. by E. Probst. McGraw, 1965.

Broadley, Mae. *Tales from the Brothers Grimm*. World Distributers, 1971.

The Brothers Grimm Popular Folk Tales, tr. by Brian Alderson, ill. by Michael Foreman. Doubleday, 1978.

The Complete Grimm's Fairy Tales, ill. by Josef Scharl. Pantheon, 1974. A reissue of the 1944 edition based on the Margaret Hunt translation. Includes a full folkloreristic commentary by Joseph Campbell and is useful to adults as well as children.

The Fisherman and His Wife, ill. by Margot Zemach. Norton, 1966.

The Four Clever Brothers, ill. by Felix Hoffmann. Harcourt, 1967.

Grimm's Fairy Tales, based on the Frances Jenkins Olcott edition of the English translation by Margaret Hunt. Follett, 1968. This beautiful edition is notable for its illustrations, which were chosen from artwork submitted by children of many nations. Frances Clarke Sayers, author and storyteller of distinction, has contributed an eloquent foreword.

Grimm's Tales for Young and Old, tr. by Ralph Manheim. Doubleday, 1977.

The Juniper Tree and Other Tales from Grimm, selected by Lore Segal and Maurice Sendak, tr. by Lore Segal with four tales tr. by Randall Jarrell, ill. by Maurice Sendak. Farrar, 1973. A two-volume edition distinguished both for the translations and the illustrations.

Rapunzel, ill. by Felix Hoffmann. Harcourt, 1961.

Rapunzel, adapted by Barbara Rogasky, ill. by Trina Schart. Hyman, Holiday, 1982.

The Seven Ravens, ill. by Felix Hoffmann. Harcourt, 1963.

The Shoemaker and the Elves, ill. by Adrienne Adams. Scribner's, 1960.

The Sleeping Beauty, ill. by Felix Hoffmann. Harcourt, 1960.

Snow-White and the Seven Dwarfs, tr. by Randall Jarrell, ill. by Nancy Ekholm Burkert. Farrar, 1972.

Tales from Grimm, freely tr. and ill. by Wanda Gag. Coward, 1936.

Copyright © 1990, Good Apple, Inc.

GA1160

Records of Grimm Tales

1. *Grimm's Fairy Tales* told by Danny Kaye—Golden Records

2. *Walt Disney's Hansel and Gretel*—Disneyland Records D.Q. 1253

3. *Hansel and Gretel*—Let's Pretend Series—Pickwick SPC 5143

4. *Hansel and Gretel and Other Grimm Tales*—Caldmon Records TC 1274

5. *Snow White and Rose Red*—Let's Pretend Series—Pickwick TG 105

6. *The Goose Girl and Sleeping Beauty*—Let's Pretend Series—Pickwick TG 105

7. *Walt Disney's Sleeping Beauty* (Songs)—Pickwick TG 109

8. *Walt Disney's Story of Sleeping Beauty*—Disneyland—MM 32

9. *Walt Disney's Cinderella* (story and songs)—Disneyland—ST-3911 MO

10. *The Bremen Town Musicians*—Let's Pretend Series—Pickwick TG 115

11. *Walt Disney's Snow White*—Disneyland—ST 3906

12. *Sleeping Beauty* told by Paul Tripp—Golden Records Childhood Productions LP 166

Copyright © 1990, Good Apple, Inc.

GA1160

This is to certify that

_____

will do everything possible
to encourage creativity,
self-expression and
love of the arts
in your children.

Copyright © 1990, Good Apple, Inc.

135

GA1160

Evaluation

I hope you have enjoyed using this book as much as I have enjoyed writing and illustrating it.

Are there other favorite stories you would like to see worked into a unit such as this? If so, I would appreciate your comments and suggestions.

. . . .

Comments:

_____

_____

_____

_____

_____

_____

Other stories I would like to see in print:

_____

_____

_____

_____

_____

_____

_____

_____

Send to:

Sister Carol Joy Cincerelli, HM
352 Elmdale Avenue
Akron, OH 44320

Copyright © 1990, Good Apple, Inc.

GA1160